WOMAN IN WHITE

BY KRISTIN DEARBORN

"Let's go back to the house." Her small voice barely broke the winter night.

He sniffed again, like he smelled something good. "You really don't smell that?"

He seemed to be gazing past the blackness (in the back of her mind she'd sort of started to realize it wasn't black, it was red.)

"I think this is blood."

James didn't answer. So she said the next piece, even though saying it out loud made it real. "I think it's Dad's blood." She could see his axe, and there—oh s-h-i-t, there sat his boots. Why his boots? It was so cold out here, he couldn't be out without boots.

"I'm going back to the house," she said.

"I'll be there in a sec. I just want to check this out."

"Check what out?" Why didn't he sound scared? Could he not see the blood? What was the smell he kept mentioning?

"Come back with me, we'll check it out tomorrow." With the police. And Mom. And maybe Dad, too. A little voice in the back of her mind suggested she shouldn't count on Dad being part of the search tomorrow.

He started to walk into the darkness. Where they stood were all deciduous trees—she'd learned about them in science class. It meant they didn't have any leaves. The bare branches let the bright moonlight spill through. James headed into a coniferous section, big old pines, whose boughs blocked the light. He headed for the shadows.

1 – DENNIS

She came out of nowhere. One minute the road was all snow, the next a woman stood in the middle of Dennis's lane. He eased down on the brake—didn't slam it—but a layer of snow covered the back road. The old Camry went into a spin and time dragged, almost to a halt. The headlights splashed light on his surroundings as he rotated.

Pine trees covered in snow.

Road.

Pine trees.

The woman wore a thin white dress and no shoes. Her feet didn't touch the ground.

That couldn't be right, must have been because of the spinning.

Dennis didn't crank the wheel, didn't mash on the brakes. He eased off the accelerator, and let the car slow and crunch to a halt in a snow bank. He hadn't been going fast to begin with, and living up here in Rocky Rhodes, Maine, you learned at an early age how to drive in the snow.

The car faced in the opposite direction, so he put it in reverse, and got himself turned back around. He'd left a Camry grill-print in the snow bank, but didn't think he'd done too much damage to the car.

The woman still stood in the road. His headlights lit her in a halo of falling snow. He put his hazards on, lighting the night in flashing orange. He reached for the door handle.

Then stopped. He had places to be. He'd had a few drinks at Sully's, and couldn't afford to deal with the cops right now, whiskey on his breath. She didn't look *right*, as if she were drifting in some other reality. A short story thrust itself in his mind; he couldn't remember the name, about a little vampire girl out in the snow. She hadn't left footprints either. When someone stopped, she'd drink their blood. It was almost enough to make him put the car back in drive and head on his way to Mary Beth Stanton's house, where she waited with beer and video games and if he was lucky, a nice warm bed.

But what would he do tomorrow when he read about the dead woman online? Could he live with that?

The answer, very nearly, was yes. He went so far as to put the car back in drive, and he almost got his foot off the brake.

She stood in the road, swaying ever so slightly. She was beautiful. Like, really beautiful.

She wasn't his problem. So wasn't his problem. He weighed the pros of seeing Mary Beth this much sooner over cons of the secret, gnawing guilt he'd likely carry with him the rest of his life if this woman died. He'd be as good as a murderer if he didn't help her.

Then he slammed the shifter up into park and got out.

In the quiet forest outside the car, the occasional glob of snow plopped from the pine boughs overhead. Winter had taken the forest and muffled it.

"Miss?" His voice sounded miserably loud and incredibly stupid.

She seemed to see him, but didn't move.

"Are you okay? Do you need a ride somewhere?" Stupid questions one and two. *Most people don't stand barefoot in a snowstorm.* Something about her, though, seemed *off*. It wasn't right. Alarm bells screamed in his mind. He'd read too many horror stories, seen too many movies, for this to be okay.

But none of that shit was *real*. This wasn't Jerusalem's Lot, this was Rocky Rhodes, the worst-named town in northern Maine. No matter how much he wished it, vampires weren't real. None of it was. The chick was probably a victim of domestic violence; some dirt bag dumped her out here and she needed to get warm and get a coat on. He thought about his own mother safely ensconced for the winter in her West Palm Beach condo, and his sister, finishing her master's in Boulder. What would he do if some dick blew past his sister if it were she standing out here?

The thought galvanized him into action. He shrugged his coat off and went to the woman. She followed his movements with dull eyes, her expression never changing. She must be in shock. He wrapped his coat around the girl's shoulders. Everything about her seemed soft, but not in a sexy way. It was as though she wasn't fully formed—Dennis cast the thought from his mind.

He led her to the car. Shivering in the cold, he opened the door for her, and helped her inside. She stared straight ahead as he hurried around to the driver's-side door. He took one last look where she'd been standing. No footprints. His coat hung on her shoulders, so she had some substance. She had to, right? In the minutes since he'd taken his coat off, snow accumulated on his shoulders and head. Snow must have covered her tracks. With accumulation like they got tonight, it made sense.

He glanced at the tracks he left, and didn't entirely buy it.

Who cared? He was freezing his ass off out here, and now he had to go all the way back to town. Mary Beth was going to be pissed. He would have called her, but he didn't have service. No one ever had service in Rocky Rhodes, not unless you went up the hill by the post office and tilted your phone just right, west toward Greenville. He could call her when he got to town, and could probably pick up a bottle of Jack to make her happy. Mary Beth loved her Jack.

He didn't want to get back in the car, but he stood in the cold wearing only a T-shirt. Something rustled out in the night, outside the normal snow sounds. Sounded like something large. He looked around, but the lights from his car only illuminated a small cone of brightness. The hazards intermittently lit the night orange. He got in, and put the car in drive, carefully executing a three-point turn to get himself turned back toward town. He glanced over at the woman. Her slack gaze led out the windshield, where the snow fell harder than ever. Dammit, if he made if back to town, he might not be able to get back out to Mary Beth's.

Oh well, he sighed in his head. *The price one pays for being the Good Samaritan.*

He headed for town.

2 – ANGELA

Angela Warren stole a sip of ice water before refilling coffees for Mark Haddon and Lou Marshall. They paused their conversation to thank her. She looked at them through her eyelashes and managed a smile as a cramp tore through her.

"Plow truck hit his car. Was stopped in the middle of River Road."

"And that's what killed him?"

"Not sure. The car was empty. Fulla blood, though."

"Whaddaya mean, full of blood?"

"It was everywhere in the car. Wasn't no body, though."

Angela pulled herself away. It looked like Beau Christie and his quiet wife Eve were ready to order. She hadn't known Dennis very well; he was three years ahead of her in school. Still, she'd known him, and it seemed strange to think he wouldn't be around anymore in his black gaming T-shirts, talking about science fiction and horror movies.

Outside, in the aftermath of last night's storm, the snow sparkled in the sun. Pretty to look at, maybe, but it couldn't entirely hide the depressed nature of Rocky Rhodes.

Eight more months in this shithole town. Then college and freedom.

"What can I get you this morning?" She plastered a smile on her face that she didn't feel.

Beau ordered for them both and Eve kept her eyes on the placemat. It wasn't a very interesting placemat—a maze and a word search in the middle, local ads all around. It hadn't been changed or updated in as long as Angela could remember, at least the past four years. She knew where every single breakfast-themed word could be found. They popped out at her now, unbidden.

"What can I get you to drink, Eve?"

"She'll have orange juice and a coffee. Thanks, darlin'." Beau ran his eyes over the front of her shirt, and she turned away. She could feel his eyes crawling over her ass. They didn't have to wear a uniform, thank god, but she got better tips when she dressed it up. She handed in the order to Jason, the cook, and went back to her ice water.

Would Beau have been checking her out if he'd known what she'd done just two short days ago? At eight weeks, the fetus is the size of a raspberry and you can already see little arms and legs.

And she'd killed it.

The bell over the door tinkled.

"Ange, why don't you take a break?" Jason came out of the kitchen and around to the front. "I got this."

Oh no. She looked up to see Nate. Handsome, rugged, football star, well-driller Nate. Angela melted into the kitchen. She heard him asking after her.

"Bad timing, bro," Jason said. "Just went on break."

"Get her."

"I think she's in the can."

"I'll wait."

"Sorry, Nate. No loitering."

"I'll order something."

"I don't serve assholes like you. Get out of here, man."

Angela leaned on the kitchen door, listening. Jason had been in both Afghanistan and Iraq. She hoped Nate wouldn't mess with him. She wouldn't want to feel responsible if Jason got arrested for kicking the crap out of Nate.

Sweat pooled between her breasts and in the small of her back. Partly because of the hot kitchen, but Nate had this effect on her.

Go away, go away, go away.

"You'll tell her I was here?" Nate asked.

Another voice chimed in. "I'm out of coffee!" That was Beau. She needed Nate to go away so she could do her job. She looked up and blinked a lot, trying to keep tears at bay.

The bell jingled again but she didn't move from her spot until Jason came back to the kitchen.

"He's gone. Beau's getting shitty about wanting a coffee refill."

"Thanks," she murmured.

Jason squeezed her shoulder with a strong hand. She couldn't look at his face, so she looked at the tattoos on his arm.

"You want me to take care of him?"

Yes. Oh, God, yes.

"Nah, he's just a pain in the ass."

"You're looking a little white."

She felt a little white. Or a lot white.

She could move away now, but that would cut into her savings. Right now she lived with Dad rent free. Anywhere else she'd start having to pay. Here she could use Dad's old Crown Vic, but he made it clear she couldn't bring it with her. Once she got to school in the fall, she'd live on campus and wouldn't need a car, but if she moved away now?

"Ange?"

"I'm okay."

"Coffee?" Beau shouted.

Angela saw Eve twitch when he raised his voice.

"I'm good, Jason, thank you."

He frowned at her, but went back to the kitchen. Angela plastered on her best Waitress Smile and took the coffee over to Beau's table.

"Jeez, Beau! Can't a girl powder her nose?"

3 - MARY BETH

Mary Beth probably shouldn't have been driving the car. But Dennis was dead.

He hadn't been her boyfriend. She was careful to escape the label—down that road lay marriage and kids and all sorts of other bullshit. Without the label, though, it meant she'd only lost "that guy she played a lot of World of Warcraft and Halo with and fucked sometimes" and it left her empty.

Ginger rode shotgun. She passed the handle of Allen's Coffee Brandy and Mary Beth took a big swig. The car swerved on the mostly clear roads and Sherri giggled from the back.

Ke$ha blasted from the car's tinny speakers. If she drank enough, if the music blared loud enough, if Sherri and Ginger didn't get too far away, she'd be all right.

"What's that?" Ginger pointed out the windshield. Mary Beth needed more washer fluid, so it was kinda hard to see, but they all looked where Ginger pointed.

"Is it a woman?" Sherri asked.

The night was dark, and the shape indistinct in the shadows. "What's she wearing?"

They were past her before they could get a good look.

"Put some clothes on, slut!" Sherri screamed out the back window. Mary Beth had no idea how Sherri could have seen what the woman wore.

By the time they got to Paradise Lost, Mary Beth had forgotten about the woman. Paradise Lost lost its liquor license, so it had been downgraded to a "Dance Hall." You had to BYOB, but Rusty, who worked the bar, had some stuff in the back you could buy under the table. Dennis hated Paradise Lost, one more too-cute name in Rocky Rhodes. He'd preferred to sit at home, lost in his online world. He liked it best when she'd been in that world with him. She did too, to be honest, but she'd fired up her computer today and let the satellite Internet fire up, logged in to WOW and found she couldn't do it. Her trailer seemed too big and too lonely.

Parking was something of a free-for-all in the Lost's dirt lot. She deposited her Subaru wagon, and the girls got out. She gazed up at the twinkling stars, glittering diamonds in the black sky. Dennis mentioned something about a meteor shower last week. He'd talked about taking her out to the old ranger station to look at it, but they'd stayed in instead. Stupid.

"The scene here is pathetic." Sherri was always such a downer. She'd spent a year at USM in Portland before dropping out, and apparently that was enough to give her a holier-than-thou complex that always seemed to come out when she drank. She fancied herself a sophisticate, but Mary Beth knew the truth—no one north of Bangor was anything close to sophisticated. You could take it a step further even and say no one north of Portland, or maybe Freeport. Summer people and ski people didn't count.

It was why Mary Beth didn't give a shit. She wanted to eat cookies for dinner? She ate cookies. Visit the gym? Rocky Rhodes didn't have one, so that was out. Who cared if she was big? Dennis hadn't. No one online did.

The patrons of the Lost were another story. She tipped up her chin and pretended she didn't care what they said about her.

Nate sat at the bar in his leather jacket, nursing a beer. It was way too cold for a leather jacket, but Nate put looking cool above all else. Ginger thought he was to die for, Mary Beth kind of thought he was a creep. Ginger sat next to him, Mary Beth took the next stool, and Sherri wandered off.

"Hey, handsome, why the long face?" Ginger asked.

As if she had to ask. Angela Warren was why the long face, she'd moved back to her dad's place. Ginger'd been railing against her all evening, calling her a bitch, a slut, saying he probably threw her out, et cetera, et cetera. But Mary Beth doubted it, and thought Ange finally smartened up and cut her losses.

Nate took Ginger in a long hug. Guys loved Ginger...until they didn't. Mary Beth tried to remember if Nate and Ginger had ever hooked up, but it was all fuzzy.

She looked away from the hug. Dennis gave the best hugs. She guzzled the coffee brandy, hoping it might keep her memories at bay. It was like she couldn't even start to process he was gone, a part of her brain assured her it wasn't true.

They hadn't found a body, that part of her brain reminded her. So not helpful. With the amount of blood in the car, finding him alive would be next to impossible. *But they said there were issues with the blood—they couldn't match it to him with 100% confidence.*

"Can I tell you something?" Nate asked Ginger. He meant his voice to be sincere, but to Mary Beth he sounded like a snake. Ginger's eyes got big and wide and she nodded, happy to be co-conspirator. Nate was talking too loud. And no one told Ginger anything. "You can't tell anyone." For the first time he acknowledged Mary Beth, too. "You can keep a secret, right?"

"I'll take it to my grave." If Nate detected the river of sarcasm in her voice, he kept it to himself.

He took a dramatic swig of his beer.

"I was going to be a father."

Oh holy shit. Ange, no.

"I threw Angie out because—" His voice broke and Ginger pounced all over that shit, but Mary Beth thought it sounded staged. "She got an abortion against my wishes. She murdered our son."

He spoke too loud. He was an asshole. Holy shit, he was an asshole. She wanted to get up and leave, but she also kind of wanted to know what he would do next.

Ginger clanked her beer down on the bar and brought both hands up to cover her mouth, let her eyes go wide. She turned and looked at Mary Beth. "Did you hear that?"

"Sure did."

"I always said there was something off about her."

"I begged her not to. I pleaded with her. Said I'd take the kid, she'd only have to carry it for nine months, then pursue whatever stupid pipe dream she has going on. She'd never have to see either one of us again." Nate hung his head, brown hair flopping over his face. He couldn't fool Mary Beth, though. She'd seen how it was starting to pull back at the temples. She couldn't think of anyone who deserved a receding hairline more than Nate Irving.

Unbidden, a memory of lying in bed with Dennis came to her. They'd been basking in the post-coital glow, lit by her old lava lamp, talking about people from when they were in school. Nate's name had come up. Dennis sure hated him. *Had* sure hated him. A lump crystalized in her throat and she tried to reconcile the fact that she would never see him again. She took a haul off the coffee brandy. Damn. She couldn't remember an omnipresent hurt like this. She hopped up off her stool and headed to the bathroom. It was a single stall, so she couldn't stay in here long. She'd always fantasized about fucking Dennis in this bathroom, him hoisting her up on the shelf, which seemed to be at the perfect height for intercourse. She didn't know if the shelf could handle her weight, but this was a fantasy.

Would only ever be a fantasy.

She let herself cry. She'd clean up the makeup on her face when she finished. She avoided looking at herself in the mirror and stood still in the middle of the room, letting the sobs take her. She didn't get too long before someone pounded on the door, braying, "I gotta pee! Let me in!"

Becca Marsh, it sounded like. Mary Beth cracked the door and let her in.

Becca, closing in on sixty and still spending every free evening at the bar—oops, *dance hall*—saw it was Mary Beth. Saw she'd been crying.

"Oh, honey." Her breath smelled like beer, but her skinny arms hugged strong, and Mary Beth let herself be taken in. She wanted to go home, but couldn't bear being alone in her trailer.

4 – ANGELA

Angela heard the car, heard the knock, but was surprised when her father poked his humorless face in her room and said, "There's a man at the door for you. You know what time it is?"

"Is it Nate?" she asked, but her father was already back in the living room parked in front of the TV. Surely he would have told her if Nate stood outside the door. Surely if it was Nate, he would have shouted at him to go to hell and slammed the door in his face. She hoped.

She peered out the little window next to the door to find... Jason? She wondered why the heck he was here. She opened the door as narrowly as she could, and squeezed outside.

Her dad was right, it was late. After eleven.

"Jason." She spoke without any warmth. "What's up?"

"I'm sorry to bug you at home."

She wrapped her arms around herself. She could see her breath in the cold night.

"Can I come in?"

She laughed at him. "No. No way."

"You want to duck in for a coat?"

"Is this going to take long?"

"I guess not." Some of the feeling vanished from his tone. She knew she was being a bitch, but she also knew the reaming she was going to get from her dad.

"I'm sorry, Jason. What's up?" She groped for a joke to make about a waitressing emergency, but came up with nothing and stayed silent.

"I just came from Paradise Lost. Nate was there. I didn't

mean to gossip, but I couldn't help overhear."

Angela's stomach contracted, drew itself in to a tight little ball. She knew what he had to tell her before he finished.

"He was loudly telling a couple of girls, Ginger, Mary Beth, some others, you aborted his child against his will."

She'd known what Jason was about to say, but hearing it? Hearing it was a whole other ballgame. She felt the color drain from her face, and the world went swimmy. Jason reached for her elbow and kept her vertical, then helped her sit on the snowy steps. He sat next to her, and she felt his warmth. She didn't look at him.

"I don't blame you," he said.

She couldn't find words. She wanted to tell him everything, to exonerate herself, but what would he think of her if she told the truth? He already knew the worst part, the punch line.

"Nate's a dirt bag. Breaking up with him, the abortion, you're on the right track."

"It doesn't feel like it," she managed.

"Yeah. It won't for a while. He'll leave you alone soon enough."

Would he, though? Unless... "You're not going to do anything, are you?"

"Do you want me to?" Jason asked. Angela tried to imagine a fight between the two of them. She didn't think Nate would last long.

Please. "No. You can't. He'll find someone else. I'm pretty sure he's had someone else on the side for a while now."

"I'd love to punch that asshole in the face."

"You can't. You can't get in trouble because of him."

"Give me the word and I'll teach him a lesson. Or just talk to him. I'm not afraid of him."

Angela did turn to look at Jason then. In his heavy coat, she couldn't see the tattoos on his neck or his arms, but she knew they were there. They'd scared her when she first met him and she hadn't looked at them. She'd been sixteen then. Finally she'd realized they were beautiful: biological and mechanical designs of what he imagined could lurk under his skin. Muscles and machines, arteries and tubing, tendons and strapping.

She shivered.

"You should go in. Sorry to bug you like this, but I thought you should know right away. Probably there won't be much blowback from this, but you never know."

Yeah right. They lived in a red pocket in an otherwise blue state. You got knocked up? You were expected to marry that man, or at least cohabitate with him until he threw you out for a younger model. Abortion was a sin. Her teeth started chattering.

"Sorry, Ange. Try and have a good night." He got up and headed for his Jeep. He paused and looked back at her, but she slipped into the house. She braced herself for her father's comment as she passed the living room doorway. She thought she'd gotten past the danger zone, almost made it back to her room.

"You certainly work fast," he said.

She pretended to ignore him and went back to her room, still decorated pink and frilly from when she'd been a girl. She wanted to tear it all down, but told herself there was no point, she'd be leaving soon—forever—in a few short months. Besides, it was like penance. She'd moved out and into Nate's place at seventeen, and stayed with him for almost two years. In retrospect it seemed like an eternity.

Her father's words rang in her ears. She didn't work fast. She'd been with one guy, and one guy only. It wasn't her fault he was such an asshole that now they were broken up other guys needed to come to her door to warn her about the things he did.

She wished Jason hadn't come. She'd rather have this one night, one more uninterrupted sleep.

People got abortions all the time. No one was going to care. People all had their own shit to deal with. She told herself they did, as she drew her frilly pink covers up to her chin.

5 - MARY BETH

The night crawled on. By one, Nate had a flock of eligible bachelorettes hating Angela Warren.

Ginger elbowed Mary Beth. "I've got some spray paint in my shed. Let's do her house."

"No. I want to get out of here. Are you coming?"

Ginger narrowed her eyes. "You're drunk. You can't drive."

"I'm fine." She wished she was drunker, but her body refused.

"I don't think so," Ginger said. "Mary Beth is drunk and won't give me her keys!"

Since when did fucking Ginger care if she drove drunk? Ginger, who didn't have a car, would have 85% fewer rides if she refused to ride with Mary Beth when she was drinking.

Nate descended on her, wrapping her in a beery hug. Mary Beth went stiff. "Let me drive you home, okay? Ginger can take your car; she'll have it back to you in the morning. You won't even know it's gone."

"No, no—"

Her keys were torn from her fingers.

"You've been through so much, honey," Becca said.

Nate, Becca, Ginger and Sherri all got Mary Beth into the passenger seat of Nate's Explorer. Every time she objected someone shushed her and hugged her. Nate could hardly get the keys in the ignition. Finally Mary Beth shut up and stared out the window, hoping the snow banks were high enough to cushion any car accident they might have.

"Dennis was a really great guy," Nate said.

She wanted to rage at him, scream at him not to use that name. "Yeah. He was."

"I hope they find out who did it."

"Yeah." They drove in silence for a bit. "Are they taking my car to spray-paint Ange's house?"

"If they are, I don't know anything about it."

She didn't believe it one bit. She hoped Angela wouldn't see the car and think she'd had anything to do with it.

Nate put the blinker on and turned down River Road. Yes, she'd come this way earlier, but she'd been distracted and with her friends (though what friends they turned out to be). He slowed the car down to a crawl. "This is right around where they found his car, right?"

She shook her head. "Just take me home."

"Is this where they found the car?"

"Somewhere around here." She didn't want to give him the pleasure of seeing her cry. She stared at her hands. At the dirt under her fingernails. She needed to stop nibbling at the skin around the edges of them. She had hideous hands, chubby fingers and thick nails. The polish on them was peeling. She'd touch it up tomorrow. She really wanted another drink.

Nate stopped the car. "I talked to my buddy Matt." Matt was a cop in Millinocket, and not nearly as much a buddy as Nate liked to think. "All they found were his shoes. They're not putting that little detail on the news, though. They think someone killed him. And they're keeping that fact to trap the killer."

"Please, Nate, let's just go."

"What do you think happened?"

"I think I'm tired and sad and want to go home."

"He was going to your house, right?"

He knew Dennis was. Nate's antagonism was fucking with her grief. She couldn't even be sad properly when he talked to her—talked at her—like this.

"If he was going to see you, does it kind of make it your fault? Like if you hadn't asked him over, he wouldn't have been on the road?"

Mary Beth gaped at him. Fought to keep her head on straight. "What do you want?"

"I don't want anything. I thought you might just like to talk about it, is all."

"Yeah, well, I don't."

Like she hadn't had that thought a thousand and one times herself. They could have played online, but she was lonely, and her back had been bothering her so she was going stir-crazy in her place. She'd wanted the company—real, physical company.

She'd been so mad when he didn't show up.

"Hey, are you okay?"

She swiped the tears away, taking pains not to smudge her makeup. Nate reached over and took her in his arms. She fought him, but he overpowered her, and he held her. He copped a feel on her tit.

"Just trying to cheer you up."

"Take me home."

"Okay, okay." He touched her tit again as he pulled away and she folded her arms over her chest. At least over two shirts and a winter coat it couldn't have been very satisfying for him.

He put the car in drive and resumed his way toward her trailer. It wasn't much farther.

"Hey, one other thing." She might get out and walk if he didn't stop talking. "If he was going to your house, why was he pointed toward town when they found the car?"

The million-dollar question. When the state police had come talk to her, they'd agreed together he must have forgotten something at home, and was going back to get it. But she couldn't for the life of her think what it might have been.

Nate pulled up in front of the trailer. Dammit, she hadn't left a light on. The place looked very dark.

"You need a hug," Nate said.

"I don't. Thanks for the ride." She spoke through gritted teeth. She reached for her door and tried to open it, but it wouldn't open.

"I control the locks and the doors in my car. Hug me, or you're not getting out. We can sit here all night. I don't have a whole lot of gas left, so it's going to get cold soon." He opened his arms. Made her come to him.

"Careful, you're going to crush me," he said.

What the hell had Angela been thinking? Two years with this?

Nate sniffed her, and kissed her cheek. "Do you want me to come in?" he asked.

God no. She shook her head. Ginger and Sherri would kill her if she ever told them she'd turned down the amazing Nate Irving. "I can make you forget all about him."

"No thanks." She hated how small her voice sounded.

"I've never been with a big girl like you."

"Not tonight, tiger." *Jesus, Mary Beth, don't antagonize him.*

"Your loss, cow."

He unlocked the door and she scrambled out of the SUV. He spun out (spraying her with slush) and headed back the way he'd come. When his headlights pulled away, it got very dark. She stood panting in the snow. What would she have done if he'd forced his way in? Stars twinkled overhead. Branches creaked and groaned, heavy with wet snow. Fear started in some deep, reptilian part of her brain. It took her two tries to get the key in the lock. There was an inch-and-a-half gap separating the steps from the door, and she always worried about dropping her keys down there. Wouldn't that be perfect tonight? She could freeze to death out here (*or be eaten by whatever's out there in the woods.*)

She told that part of her brain to shut up. She'd lived here all her life, and she knew there were bears, coyotes, the occasional wolf down from Canada, bobcats, and once in a blue moon, a mountain lion. She also knew the moose and the deer were more dangerous. Mess with a rutting moose and you wouldn't make that mistake a second time. Nothing in the woods would eat her.

She got the door open and spilled into her living room, slamming it behind her. She turned on all the lights and slept on the couch. Her bed held too many memories.

6 – LEE

"Isn't that an ice cream?" asked LeeAnne Dudley.

Vince Staghorn glowered at her. She knew he wanted to laugh, but was trying to be *professional*.

"It's a city up north. Between Greenville and Millinocket."

"There are cities between Greenville and Millinocket?"

"Lee, come on."

"Sorry. You're serious, though, that between Greenville and Millinocket, there is a city called Rocky Rhodes?"

"Yes, though I guess it's not actually a city. Hovel is more like it, from what they tell me."

"And I have to go there?"

"Yes."

Lee sighed and flipped her blonde hair back. She didn't have to head so far north very often. That was because she was a forensic chemist, and since not many people lived north of Bangor, there weren't a lot of forensics that needed examination.

"When?"

"Tomorrow."

"Why are you telling me this now?"

They were in her bed in her tiny bohemian Portland apartment. Neither of them wore a thing, and they wrapped around each other like vines. She absolutely loved that she was fucking a guy named Staghorn. So what if he was married? To someone who was most certainly not her.

"Because I have good news."

"Oh Jesus, it gets better than Rocky Rhodes, Maine, in January? What's next?"

"They're sending me up there too."

"Oh." It stopped her in her tracks. A whole night with him. A whole car ride with him, maybe. Suddenly she hoped for all sorts of terrible things to happen to the little hovel, so they'd have to stay a very long time.

"Kathy did the analysis, but she's got a personal conflict, and doesn't want to go. I sort of volunteered you." This happened a lot—being single and childless, Lee got to do lots of things the others in the office didn't have to do. Such was the price for her freewheeling life.

"Thanks." She kissed him. As she pulled away, she caught him glancing at the digital clock on the dresser. They didn't have any lights on and as the daylight faded, the room grew dim.

"I gotta go," he said.

"I know." She reached over and flicked on the light. Warm tapestries covered the walls and the ceiling. She'd plastered them over hideous wallpaper—a repeating design of doves and flowers.

"Don't cover up." He pulled the sheet away from her and she caught herself thinking about his wife. She banished the thought. He pulled on his uniform—the only thing that got her hotter than Staghorn was Staghorn in his trooper's uniform.

"Grete will give you the lowdown on Rocky Rhodes when you get in tomorrow."

"Are you going to ride up with me?"

His pause answered her question. "Not sure yet. We'll see."

Sounded like a big fat no. Whatever. She had loads of audio books on her iPhone. She commuted from Portland to Augusta most days, and had plenty of time to listen.

When Vince left, her tiny apartment felt huge, vacant. Gaping and empty. Oh wait, maybe that wasn't the apartment, maybe that was her.

Tomorrow night, she told herself. She wouldn't be going to bed alone. It thrilled her more than she wanted it to.

She rolled herself up in a quilt and dragged her laptop over, booted it up and googled "Rocky Rhodes, Maine." She found a Google map, a Wikipedia page, a bunch of black-and-white pictures of a quaint downtown and some trains. The Weather

Channel. She clicked the link, and wished she hadn't. Current temperature: -11º F. Lucky for her, tomorrow's weather was warmer, only -5. A couple days of that, then snowflakes all over the place. She didn't even know what the crime was, or why they couldn't send their samples to the lab like most people did.

She thought about Vince, getting home to his wife and their two kids.

"Nope," she told herself, and hauled out her phone. She texted friends until she found a few people to go have dinner and drinks with. If she was headed into the North Maine woods, she wasn't spending her last night in civilization alone.

7 – TESSA

"Go and tell your father it's time for dinner." Mom stood at the stove. Everything smelled fantastic and Tessa couldn't wait to eat.

"You heard her," Tessa said to her brother, James. "Go get Dad."

"She meant you, stupid." James was eight. What a pain.

"I meant both of you. Coats, hats, boots, gloves. It's cold out."

"Can I stay and help you set the table?" Tessa asked. It was dark out and it was cold out, and she'd had a really long walk back from the bus this afternoon.

"I'm not going if she's not going." Sometimes she hated her brother. He always ruined things for her, just for the sake of being awful. Over and over her mother explained the big sister's job is one of unending patience, that someday her brother will need her and she will rise to the challenge, and when they're both grown, they'll be very close. Mom talked to her brother every day.

"Isn't he way out in the woods?" Tessa asked.

"Not *way* out. You can follow the tracks from his sled."

Tessa paused for a moment, debating whether to make a stink or to be a good example. She decided, like she almost always did, on the latter. She guessed that in the history of all young girls, there had never been one who'd been so good, but who wanted so badly to be bad. She dutifully shut the TV off, and started bundling up.

"How cold is it?"

"Really cold. Go get him and come right back."

"But exactly how cold?"

"It's zero degrees."

Tessa rolled her eyes and wrapped a scarf around her neck, covering her nose and mouth.

Mom ushered them out into the snowy evening. The sun was gone, but the moon had taken its place, and shone almost as bright. It reflected off the snow and cast long, sharp shadows. Its light dimmed the stars. Somewhere a dog barked, probably at the Masons' farm. The bark sounded frustrated, insistent.

"Thanks a lot," Tessa snapped.

"It's your own fault."

"You can't be trusted out here on your own."

James shrugged, his bundled shoulders rising and falling. Snow crunched under their boots. Their father was out gathering firewood, and had hauled a kid's sled behind him to help carry it back. Other kids' dads got wood delivered in trucks, but not her dad. He said he wasn't about to pay for something he had ten acres of in his backyard.

Aside from the barking dog, the woods were quiet. And cold. The kind of cold that freezes the little hairs in your nostrils and makes your breath puff out in a big cloud of steam. Tessa walked behind James and pretended she to smoke a cigarette, blowing her breath out in big, dramatic puffs.

"Dad!" James shouted.

Tessa looked back. They'd barely even entered the woods. The house looked so warm and inviting, all the windows lit yellow, the Christmas lights still up and glowing along the gutters.

"Hey, Dad, it's dinner!"

The dog paused its barking for a moment, and the woods went silent. Tessa's skin crawled. Her parents always stressed how big the woods were here—start off in the wrong direction and you could walk until you died without seeing another person.

They made sure to stick to the sled trail. Tessa's toes were starting to get numb, and she couldn't see the house anymore. Fear inched up her spine.

"Hey, James, slow down."

"If I slow down, I'm going to freeze to death."

Gosh, he might be right. She hurried to catch up with him.

"Hey, Dad!" James shouted again.

Tessa looked back and couldn't see the house. Only the trail her father had worn, with his big boots and the little sled. Still looking back, she smacked into her brother, who'd stopped in the middle of the trail.

"What?" she snapped, frightened, though she couldn't say why. Then she turned. She saw her dad's sled, sitting in a clearing, with fallen trees all around. Everything was dark, though. Not shadows. Something black and liquid coated the snow. Tessa took a step back.

"Do you smell that?" James didn't sound scared, he sounded enchanted.

She did smell something, but it was an awful scent, coppery and cloying.

James took a step away from her and she stumbled forward.

"Let's go back to the house." Her small voice barely broke the winter night.

He sniffed again, like he smelled something good. "You really don't smell that?"

He seemed to be gazing past the blackness (in the back of her mind she'd sort of started to realize it wasn't black, it was red.)

"I think this is blood."

James didn't answer. So she said the next piece, even though saying it out loud made it real. "I think it's Dad's blood." She could see his axe, and there—oh s-h-i-t, there sat his boots. Why his boots? It was so cold out here, he couldn't be out without boots.

"I'm going back to the house," she said.

"I'll be there in a sec. I just want to check this out."

"Check what out?" Why didn't he sound scared? Could he not see the blood? What was the smell he kept mentioning?

"Come back with me, we'll check it out tomorrow." With the police. And Mom. And maybe Dad, too. A little voice in the back of her mind suggested she shouldn't count on Dad being part of the search tomorrow.

He started to walk into the darkness. Where they stood were all deciduous trees—she'd learned about them in science class. It meant they didn't have any leaves. The bare branches let the bright moonlight spill through. James headed into a coniferous section, big old pines, whose boughs blocked the light. He headed for the shadows.

"James, come on," she said. "You can have the TV tonight." He didn't stop. "You can have the TV all week."

He paused. "I'll just be a second. Wait right there for me."

"I want to go back."

"There's something out here."

That's what she was afraid of. But she was the big sister; it was her responsibility to get him inside.

"Dammit, James!" She made her voice as sharp and mean as Mom did sometimes.

"Thirty seconds," he said.

Then the dark swallowed him.

She started to shiver and she had to pee. A frigid breeze sliced the night, causing the boughs to creak and groan. Tears froze on her cheeks. She wanted to call to him, but the words caught in her throat. Once it finished with him, it would come after her next.

Her pulse pounded in her ears. She wouldn't have to call out, it would hear her heart beat.

Where James vanished, a pine tree shifted and discharged its load of snow with a loud thump. Tessa squeaked and ran, following her dad's sled trail, running as fast as she could. Her foot caught some ice and she slipped, falling on her hands and knees. She couldn't help it—hot wetness splashed down her leg. It made her cry harder as shame washed over her. First the pee was so hot it steamed, then it started to freeze on her clothes. She struggled up and finally saw the warm yellow lights of the house. Her lungs screamed from running and from the cold. She threw open the door.

"Finally! I was about to send out a search party. Go wash up for—" Then her mother turned around and saw her, covered in snow, wild-eyed and terrified.

"Theresa, what happened? Where's James? Where's Daddy?"

Tessa started to blubber.

James said thirty seconds—he should be along any minute

now, right? And he'd have Dad with him, 'cause that's obviously what he went to find, right?

She tried to talk, but couldn't force the words out. Her mother pulled on a coat, LL Bean boots.

"No!" Tessa managed.

Mom stopped and looked at her.

"You can't go out there!"

"What happened?"

She shook her head. "I don't know."

"Where's your father?"

"I don't know! You need to call the police."

"Is he hurt?"

She nodded. "I think so."

"Badly?"

More nodding.

"James?"

"I don't know. He went into the woods. He said he'd be right back."

Mom moved for the door again.

"No! There's something out there. It's going to get you, too."

"Someone's out there?"

"No, some*thing*!"

Mom stepped out into the night.

8 – ANGELA

"What the hell did you do?"

Angela had her work clothes on and sat finishing a bowl of Cheerios at the island in the kitchen when her father came in from outside. He stomped the snow off his boots and set them by the woodstove.

"What do you mean what did I do?"

"The house was vandalized."

The milk went sour in her mouth. She wanted to spit it out, but she swallowed it, forcing it down a tight throat. "Vandalized how?"

"Spray paint. In red. Says *slut* and *murderer*."

Angela fought her fingers to keep hold of the bowl of cereal. She set it on the counter, then found a stool to sit on.

Murderer. She wasn't. It was a fetus. The size of a raspberry.

"This have to do with that fella went missing on River Road?"

She shook her head. Jason was right. Nate was telling people. The town talked. She should consider herself lucky her father didn't already know.

"Dad, sit down."

He narrowed his eyes at her.

Swallowing felt like sandpaper. "I broke up with Nate because I got an abortion. He didn't want me to do it. Wanted me to have the baby."

Now would come the lecture on sex. On getting what she deserved.

"Sounds like it was the smart thing to do."

Wait, what?

"He's really mad about it. And Jason—the guy last night? —he overheard Nate telling a bunch of girls about it at the bar."

"I've half a mind to go teach that little punk a lesson."

Dad and Jason could go together.

"Do you want me to?" he asked. "I could get Brick Adams to come with me." Brick was a nearly retired state trooper, and one of her dad's close friends.

"I want to keep my head down until I can move away."

"August is a long time."

"I know."

He didn't come to her side or hug her, but he nodded to her, and coming from him, that nod meant a lot. She gave him a half smile, and he headed off into the living room, settled into his chair, and turned on the TV.

9 – LEE

"It's a tiny town," they told her. "You and Vince can handle it."

Lee rolled her eyes. She hated driving the mobile crime lab. If someone else came to drive the thing, though, she wouldn't get any time alone with Vince. They were guaranteed at least one night. He'd promised her that they'd spend one night after driving the three hours to get there. When she looked at the map, it seemed so far away, but three hours wasn't really that long. It took about that long to get to her sister's summer house in Hyannis, if she went at night when there wasn't a lot of tourist traffic. Luckily the weather for today was clear. Tomorrow was another story. Before they left, she made Vince promise her he wouldn't leave her in Rocky Rhodes. He'd laughed and told her he wished he could kiss her. The rule was not at work. She was pretty sure no one even suspected them. They were very discreet.

She pulled the RV into the Cedar Pines Motel. Cedars weren't pines, They might as well have a Maple Aspen Motel. Stupid. After she checked in at the motel she would drive the RV to meet Vince at the crime scene.

Lee headed in to the nondescript, flat building. She couldn't recall ever seeing a motel so boring and uninspired. The lobby—if you could call it that—boasted an ancient sun-bleached leather couch parked in front of a big window, and a small empty desk. She suspected there was no continental breakfast here. She'd tried to convince Vince they should spend the night in the casino in Bangor, but he didn't go for it, he called it a waste of the taxpayers' money. "As much of a waste as getting two rooms but only using one?" she asked. He hadn't laughed.

The walls were plastered with hunting, fishing and snow-mobiling pictures. God, she couldn't wait to get out of here.

"Hello," she called.

"One sec, hon."

Oh boy, Lee Dudley loved to be called hon. She sat on the couch and looked out at the RV. She picked at a piece of clear packing tape over a rip.

"Can I help you, hon?" A stout woman came to the desk. If Lee looked in the dictionary, this woman's picture would sit beside the word *matronly*.

"Hi. I need two rooms for tonight." Lee gave their names and got two keys—real, honest-to-goodness keys. The motel phone rang, and the woman ignored it, picking up Lee's company credit card. Jesus, did they even take credit cards here?

The phone rang and rang, not bumping over to voice mail.

"Are you going to answer that?"

"When I'm finished with you."

"I'll wait."

The woman gave her a distrustful look, but answered the phone. Lee looked at her phone and the discouraging NO SERVICE written across the top.

The woman looked up at Lee. Frowned at her. Peered at the name on the credit card.

"Are you LeeAnne Dudley?" she asked.

"Yes." That was what the card said.

She held out the receiver with a chubby hand. The cord stretched. Lee blinked at it, but accepted the offering.

"Hello?"

"We've got another scene."

Vince. "Another scene? Are you kidding?"

"No, I'm going to give you an address. I need you to get over here as fast as you can."

"I need your pen, please," she said to the matronly woman. She took forever to hand over the Bic. Lee wrote on her hand as Vince spoke.

"I'll be there as soon as I finish checking in."

He hung up without saying good-bye.

"I suspect you're here about the disturbance at the Carey place?"

"I can't say," she said, though really she could if she wanted to.

"An awful lot of disappearances around here these past few weeks." She ran the card by taking a rubbing of it and dialing the number in on a keypad. Lee's cell phone could have done it faster.

"Oh yeah?" Lee asked.

"Dennis Clarke, the Careys, Aziz Eliot, Clarence Tebbs."

She didn't know about Eliot. Tebbs was the first; he'd been reported missing after a snowstorm. He'd been at his camp and no one had heard from him for days. When a plow finally made it down his camp road, his friends found the door hanging open, a frozen pot of beans on the stove, and an awful lot of blood in the living room. They could have had Clarke's car towed down to Augusta, but since they needed to come up to Tebbs's camp, they figured they'd do the car when they got up here. Now a third site? And a fourth missing person.

"You said his name was Aziz Eliot?" There weren't a lot of Azizes in this part of the state.

The matron nodded, and passed her a slip to sign. She jotted Eliot's name on her hand, and signed her name for the rooms. In the RV she punched the address on the GPS and let the computer guide her to her destination. On the way she had to stop twice to let snowmobiles cross the road. Maybe this was *real* Maine, but she didn't give a shit. When she got home—back to Portland—she was going to take a week in Boston. No, Boston wasn't big enough. She wanted to go to New York to get this taste of hickdom out of her bones.

10 – ANGELA

Angela was glad about her opening shift the next morning. She couldn't face the idea of walking into the diner through a sea of people who judged her. Somehow it was better if they came in one by one. Jason was already there when she arrived, and yellow lights lit up the diner in the darkness. The big red sign wasn't on yet, but without it, without judgmental patrons, she had the illusion of the diner being a nice place. A homey place.

"Good morning!" he called from the kitchen, when she used her key to let herself in.

He stepped into the dining room and thrust a hot mug of coffee in her hands. "Jessalynn isn't coming in."

"I didn't think she would. Have they found Frank or her son?"

"No. They've got the mobile crime lab up from Augusta, but I don't think they found much."

Angela wondered what they could tell about the spray paint on her house.

"I think it's going to be busy," he said. "Another fucking storm is rolling in, and by this time tomorrow we'll all be snowbound."

She groaned. The diner would be slammed today, and she'd be expected to be here tomorrow, too. Anyone who managed to make it in tomorrow would be irritable and nasty.

"I have four-wheel drive if you need a ride home."

He smiled at her, and she dropped her eyes. She didn't want men smiling at her. Probably ever again. She wanted to go to school and lose herself in books and studying and facts. There would be no time for dates if she spent every day in the library from sunup until midnight. She'd heard there was a café inside the library there, so she wouldn't even have to leave for meals. Just for the classes.

"How was your night after I left? Sorry to barge in like I did. Your dad seemed pretty pissed."

Tell him? Don't tell him? She didn't want his pity and his anger, but she also didn't want him hearing about it from someone else when the next customer came in.

"Someone spray-painted my house." She clutched the coffee, so hot it almost burned her hands. She liked the hurt right now. She stared at its oil-slick surface.

"Are you kidding me?"

"No." She couldn't even imagine what she would have said to him if she were kidding. "I had a great night after you left. You know, after you told me about my ex outing me about my abortion." *My abortion.* Even after having one, the words didn't seem to fit her.

She couldn't look up at him. She didn't want to see the rage creeping through him, a bit of red around the tattoos that poked up under his collar.

"I can help you," he said.

She shook her head.

Something hit the glass from outside. Beau and Eve Christie. It was early still, they weren't open yet. They both looked at the clock on the wall, 5:50 a.m., they didn't open until six, but it was cold outside and Jason stalked past her to open the door for them.

"Morning, folks. Just a warning, not everything is quite up and running yet. Take a seat wherever you'd like."

"Coffee?" Angela echoed, with a smile.

"You know it," Beau boomed, stomping snow off his boots. Eve followed him, slinking like an alley cat. She took her place across from him and pulled her rosary from her pocket. Beau shut her out with the *Bangor Daily News.* Some mornings Eve brought her Bible, some days she ran the beads through her finger, muttering to herself. Today looked like a muttering morning.

Jason filled their coffee cups, even though it was supposed to be Angela's job.

"That's a mighty pretty rosary, ma'am," he said. Angela couldn't see it from where she stood, pulling the money from the little safe and filling the register for the day. If Eve Christie had it, it must be pretty. The woman wore a skirt even today. Nate used to say cruel things about her, debating whether Jesus or Beau Christie would be a better husband. Angela noticed something boiling behind the woman's startled eyes. One of these days she wasn't going to take her husband's crap anymore.

"Fucking page five." Beau slammed the paper down, sloshing the coffee. Eve jumped like she'd been goosed.

"That's the fourth disappearance in this goddamn town, and it's only on page five." He brandished the front page—the Bangor waterfront slicked with ice. "This is what they think is newsworthy? It's winter. It's Maine. It's snowing. That's not goddamn news."

Each time Beau cursed, Eve twitched like she'd been shocked. Angela tried to keep her eyes on the register. Jason unlocked the door, and disappeared into the kitchen. She felt so alone out here, almost abandoned. What a stupid way to feel, she told herself, and pushed the thoughts away.

"Are you ready, Beau, or do you need a few more minutes?"

Beau liked to order the same thing every day, the Lumberjack Breakfast, with three eggs, three strips of bacon, three sausage links, three pancakes, hash browns and wheat toast. The only time he didn't order it was when she asked, "The usual?" Then he would huff at her, and choose something else.

"Five more minutes? And more coffee!"

"Whatever you need, Beau."

The bell above the door tinkled, and Angela's heart leapt into fight-or-flight mode. *Don't be Nate. Please don't be Nate.*

It wasn't. She didn't recognize the two people who walked in, but she knew who they were. A state trooper and a beautiful woman—she had to be the forensics expert they'd brought in to look at the blood. Even though it was five past six in the morning, her white-blonde hair was blow-dried and pulled back into a bouncy ponytail, and her subtle makeup made her brown eyes pop.

They took a booth near the door, and the trooper pulled his hat off.

"Angela!" Beau, it seemed, was ready to place his order. She went to him and jotted down his Lumberjack Breakfast request, careful not to prompt him, lest he change his mind. Eggs scrambled and runny, strawberry jam on the toast, bacon undercooked. She turned to Eve.

"Just the coffee," she murmured.

"Bullshit just the coffee. Order a real goddamn breakfast." Beau turned to Angela. "She wonders why we can't have any fucking kids. She's got to eat something."

"The oatmeal is really good," Angela suggested.

"She's not going to have bullshit oatmeal."

The state trooper watched them from across the room.

"Get her Bob's Breakfast."

Angela knew better than to check with Eve and jotted it down on her pad.

"I'll be back with more coffee in a few minutes."

"Good."

She went out back to hand the order off to Jason.

"I'm going to punch that guy in the goddamn mouth one of these days," Jason muttered to the griddle.

"It's not worth it."

"I know, but it's to fun fantasize about my fist hitting his chin."

Angela went to the trooper's table, and took their order.

"Is he a regular?" The trooper cut his eyes to Beau.

"Oh yeah. Every morning. When he doesn't come in, we get worried. That's his booth over there, and you should see if someone else sits in it."

"He sounds like a lovely guy," said the woman. "I kinda wish he'd be lovely at a lower volume."

"I can talk to him," the trooper said.

"No. Not worth it." She smiled, and ordered an orange juice.

The bell tinkled again while Angela poured the drinks. Her heart seized, but not as badly. Nate couldn't do too much to her with a state trooper sitting there.

She turned to see Sherri Walker take a seat at the counter.

"Hi, I'll be with you in a sec."

She made it back around to Sherri, beginning to wish they had someone to cover Jessalynn.

Angela opened her mouth to take the girl's order, but she held up a hand to stop her.

"Where's Jason?"

"He's in the back. He's cooking."

"He can take my order. I'm not going to talk to a murdering whore."

Angela felt her jaw go slack and knew she was gaping. People were looking at her, so she nodded, and disappeared into the kitchen.

"Busy morning?" Jason asked, scooping Beau's disgusting runny scrambled eggs onto a plate.

"Sherri needs you to take her order." Once she said it aloud, she realized how stupid it sounded, and how she shouldn't have nodded. She *should* have explained that she was the waitress, and Jason was the cook, if she couldn't give her order to the waitress, then she wouldn't be able to eat.

"What?" His tone was icy.

A floodgate of panic opened above her and tons of it rained over her. She felt like she was drowning in it. She was so stupid.

"What's wrong?" Jason peered out the front. He saw Sherri and his face fell. "Here." He thrust a spatula in her hand. "Pancakes are almost ready to flip. Ten more seconds max."

She couldn't see Sherri from where she stood, but she could see Jason, and the trooper behind him. They both frowned. God, what had she been thinking? Now Jason thought she was a fool.

The first of her tears sizzled on the griddle beside Beau Christie's pancakes.

11 – LEE

L ee couldn't tell what the girl said to the waitress, but she had seen the girl's face fall, and saw the smoking-hot tattooed chef come stalking out. He moved like a man with military training, and she didn't like his ponytail, but she could appreciate a good-looking dude.

"What is up with this place?" She kept her voice low.

"Small-town stir-crazy? End of January's about when it starts setting in."

Her mind kept drifting back to the blood she'd been looking at. She'd never seen anything like it. She'd be calling this morning to bring a team up. There was a lot of it, but something had broken down all the DNA. Usually she could finger bleach as a likely suspect, but there was no trace of that. No trace of anything but oddly impotent blood. And so much of it. They were inclined to assume the disappeared weren't still alive after losing so much, but they could be—the blood was human, but she couldn't tell anything else about it. And there were no bodies. No body, no crime.

They'd gotten back to their rooms a bit after three last night. Vince was too tired for any funny business, but had come to her room and immediately passed out, snoring like a chain saw. After an hour of that, she'd prized the key from his uniform pants pocket and gone to sleep in his room. It wasn't at all what she'd expected, and she surprised herself by crying. It was supposed to be some Podunk easy-to-solve murder; she'd so had her heart set on a real night with him. And the snoring, Jesus god, she could still hear it, albeit faintly, through the wall.

The cute cook kept his voice low so they couldn't hear the

girl at the counter get her dressing-down. She looked a little skanky, and wore flannel pajama pants. Lee hated, hated,
hated when people wore PJ pants out of the house. So trashy.
Lee wasn't interested in leaving without a full beauty treat-
ment every morning. She even showered before morning fitness
classes. No one can see what a good person someone is at first
glance. Might as well let them enjoy the inside and the out.

"She's not touching my food." Trashy girl raised her voice.
She sounded as though she'd been up all night smoking.

"Sherri. She's the waitress, I'm the cook. If you don't like
that, the door is right there." He pointed.

Sherri looked around the restaurant. Made eye contact with
each of the four patrons in turn.

"Fine. I'm leaving. I'm not having some baby killer touch my
food."

Lee saw Vince sit up straighter. He had kids, he loved kids,
he saw himself as champion of all children. He looked like a
dog that'd seen something worth attacking.

"Keep your voice down," the cook growled.

"She murdered Nate Irving's unborn son. She went to the
abortion doctor in Bangor without even telling anyone. She's
not touching my food!"

Sherri stalked out. As she left, Lee caught a whiff of pot and
cheap perfume.

Vince relaxed. They'd gone around and around on the abortion issue. He didn't like it, but respected it was legal. The cook
stalked off back to the kitchen.

"It's like breakfast and a show," Lee said.

"Too bad we've got places to be."

She took it a little personal, sure they had places to be, but
they were out, together. It didn't happen very often. She commanded herself to enjoy it.

When the waitress came back, she moved like a mouse. A
broken little creature afraid to create trouble.

"Can I take your order?" she mumbled.

Vince wouldn't look at her.

"I'm so sorry," Lee said.

The girl shook her head. "It's—whatever. Thanks."

They ordered.

Their conversation dried up as it began to snow outside. Serious weather headed their way and if they didn't get out soon they may find themselves stuck here. But still more blood samples, more analysis to do. She pulled out her phone to look at her weather app, but she didn't have any bars, and the place didn't have Wi-Fi. Her sleek iPhone was a brick here. She wondered how these people lived, then reminded herself most of them likely didn't know what they were missing. These folks thought of a trip to Bangor as a trip to the city.

The waitress brought food for the loud guy and his wife. Lee's stomach grumbled. The girl vanished back into the kitchen. The bell rang as a group of men came in, stomping off the cold. They were all talking about the coming snow. She hated the snow. Hated the cold. Hated Vince right now, sitting over there, smug and ignoring the poor waitress. She couldn't remember the last time she was so interested in leaving a place.

"Eat it."

God, the asshole in the corner raised his voice again. This time at his poor wife. She had to be his wife, the way she cowered in front of him. It wasn't right. Obvious domestic abuse, why wasn't Vince shitting a brick about that?

"I said fucking eat it! I paid for it."

These folks were out of Lee's sight lines, and she really wanted to turn to look, but didn't want to be rude. Wasn't this bullshit clouding her unbiased scientific analysis of the crime scene? She hated almost everyone in the town (the cook was pretty cute, and he'd stood up for the waitress) and had no inclination to try to figure out what was killing them.

The thought went too far and she felt bad for it.

She stared down at her table, a generic diner pattern with little interlocking boomerangs of blue and pink. It reminded her of old 3-D, like if she put some glasses on a 3-D pattern would emerge from the Formica. Soon she would be back in Portland (or even Augusta or Bangor), back in civilization.

Lee did turn when she heard the crash of a plate breaking. The heavy man gaped at his wife.

"I said I'm not eating it. I'm not coming back here. This place is sinful."

Lee and Vince shared a look. His radio went off. Some kind of a situation on the outskirts of town.

"Bring me with you," she said.

"I can't. I'll let you know if we need the RV."

"You're kidding me. I'll sit in the car, I'll—"

"Gotta go." He got held up at the door as the wife hurried out, the husband on her trail. Assholes didn't pay for their meals. In the new quiet, Lee heard the waitress crying in the kitchen.

12 – Beau

Anger boiled Beau Christie's blood. He'd heard the expression before, but today, embarrassed and retreating from the only restaurant in town, he truly understood it. He didn't even feel the cold as they stepped into the gray morning.

She knew better than to fuck with him like this. Eve, in the low heels she always wore, damn the weather, walked ahead of him toward the car. Bitch was speed-walking this morning.

"Eve, slow down or you'll fall on your ass."

She didn't indicate she'd heard him.

His wife reached the car, and kept walking. Kept walking. It almost didn't register in his infuriated brain at first. Who did she think she was?

He jogged to catch up to her, his heart pounding in his ears. He wasn't a jogger, and the fact that she'd made him do it made him so mad he could taste it—an iron-like flavor.

He caught her arm and she wobbled and almost lost her balance. This shit city barely did anything to clear the sidewalks. Just because the schools were closed, the utilities thought they could take a day off. She slipped on the ice, and his vice grip on her arm held her up.

"Where do you think you're going?"

She turned and looked at the Catholic church, a one-story building with a pathetic half steeple, built sometime in the seventies.

"I have to pray."

"There's no one there. Not in this weather."

"It's always unlocked. I need to be in the presence of the Lord."

"You need to get your ass home with me."

"No, Beau, I do not."

He knew he couldn't hit her here. He wasn't stupid, he knew the bullshit liberals didn't approve of any kind of physical education—you couldn't even hit a dog when it needed to be taught.

"Come on back to the car."

The trooper stood in the doorway of the diner, watching them. He jammed his hands into his pockets.

"That little harlot's been serving us I don't know how long. She touches my food every day. And you wonder why we can't have a child? We don't deserve one, the den of sin we live in." He didn't speak. Couldn't come up with words. "I have to pray."

Bitch turned her back on him.

He needed to teach her. Had to come up with something to make her regret this, and with the trooper standing a hundred feet away, he had to be creative.

"Go pray. Your ride home is leaving now."

She turned. "A half hour…"

"Ride's leaving. You can pray or come home where you belong." *And learn a lesson or two once you get there.* He didn't say that part out loud. He didn't need to. She knew.

"I'm sorry, Beau. I have to pray."

"I'll see you at home then."

She didn't even have the nerve to say anything to him. She just kept going, speed-walking in her low heels, making for the church.

Beau stalked back to his Town Car and fired up the engine. He let it warm up as he watched her walk away from him.

A quick glance told him the trooper was still around, taking his sweet-ass time getting in his car. Beau eased away from the curb, pretending this wasn't a rude shock. As if he'd planned all along to be abandoned by his wife this morning.

He pulled car from the curb, and eased onto the street. The snow lay a slick layer of white down over the roads, and he found himself fighting the car to keep it on the road. Once he turned down West Hill Road, things got worse. His were the only set of tracks on the now-white road surface.

The big car fishtailed, and he cursed it. Then he smelled…

something, and Eve flitted from his mind.

He couldn't put words to the smell, but instantly he felt like a man. Eve didn't let him feel that way very often, not since it became pretty clear they weren't going to be parents. He eased the Town Car to a stop and rolled the window down.

The smell rushed in, carrying snowflakes with it. He put the car in park and got out. The sky was lighter, day had broken, but dawn would never come today.

The smell reminded him of expensive perfume and... pussy?

"Hello?" he shouted. He stood on the edge of a flat, wide field. In the fall, Chris Barrett harvested hay here, rolling up big hay bales that looked like cinnamon rolls. He left the Town Car door open, keys in the ignition. It made an obnoxious dinging sound, but he left it. He'd be right back anyway. He couldn't see anyone out there in the field. A smell like that, though—there was bound to be a prize at the other end.

A sliver of reason asked him what he expected to find out there. A beautiful sex-scented, perfumed woman ripe for the taking?

It wouldn't teach Eve a lesson, but he could work with it. A change might be nice. He loved his wife, and would never go so far as to take a mistress. But one roll in the hay out here...? He chuckled at his own joke.

The reasonable voice asked him if he really meant to have sex with a strange woman in a field. He shoved it away, and breathed in the sex smell on the wintery air. He picked up his pace. He wasn't a jogger, no, but he surely hustled now over the uneven ground.

Where was she?

A hint of panic filtered in around the edges of his thoughts. He peeked back over his shoulder, made sure he could still see the car and it was okay. Then he pushed on. The smell grew stronger. Need swirled in him, cooked inside him. He huffed and wheezed. Sweat broke out all over his body and the winter winds froze it. He began to shiver. He didn't care. The need to rut filled him. Made him shake.

There. Against the tree line. Oh Jesus, there she was, and

she was beautiful. She wore a white slip over milky skin. Long arms, coltish legs. He wanted to run his hands over every inch of her. Run his mouth over her.

His heart threatened to explode from his chest, pounding and surging in him. His pulse and the vision of the woman filled him. He wondered what her name was and how her eyes could be so black.

He was so close, maybe twenty feet away, when he stepped wrong, the tip of his shoe catching a gopher hole. He fell, and the impact sent waves of pain through his whole body. He lay on the icy, hard ground trying to catch his breath. An aftershock, pain started in his chest and radiated out through him, seeming to centralize in his left arm.

He recognized it. He'd been here before. He knew he needed to get to a doctor. He carried a satellite phone for this very reason, but it sat snugly in the Town Car's cup holder, full battery, ready to make a call.

The car seemed a million miles away, a tiny navy blue speck in a white world.

Adrenaline flooded him. What was he doing? This was stupid. The whole situation was stupid. Why couldn't he just let his wife pray?

Beau turned back to the woman, meaning to ask her to help him.

She wasn't there. In her place hovered an indistinct blob, almost female in shape. Wind rustled what might have looked like a white dress, and it drifted toward him. And behind it? Words couldn't describe the thing behind the shape. *Huge* and *looming, female* and *hungry* came close.

Panic brought another wave of pain, and Beau found he didn't even have the breath for a scream. The thing inched closer and the snowy morning went all white. Was this the light they all talked about? Where was Eve's god now? If it was a good god, why had it abandoned him?

The white became blackness as Beau's heart gave out.

The thing in the forest stopped. It did not experience emotions, but if it had, this would be disappointment. The thing before it was dead, of no use to it now. It could not feed off the dead. It retreated into the trees, its hunger growing.

13 – LEE

Lee paid the tab for the assholes who'd walked out. Jason had argued, saying he'd take care of it, but she insisted, and he eventually caved and took her wad of cash. She sat, poking at her breakfast, watching the snow. She kept looking at her useless phone as though she thought this time it might show some signal. It didn't. She had a radio, but it sat out in the truck. Snow fell in thick sheets, silent. It accumulated on the road. She wanted to be back in the hotel room. She wanted to go back to bed. With Vince. She rubbed at her eyes, careful not to smudge her makeup.

Her job today was to wait around until someone gave her the go-ahead to either go back south (yes please, she hoped very much it would be this option) or if there was another crime scene, she could check out the blood.

She thought about what they'd found last night. The big blood splotches on the snow. It should have been what she thought of as she fell asleep, not anger at how close and how far Vince had been from her. If she loved him, she should have put up with the snoring. You could get used to anything, right?

She stopped her thoughts in their tracks. Love had nothing to do with what she and Staghorn had. It was all pure, animal lust.

She could hear the hot cook talking to the poor waitress, a soft indistinct murmur.

She thought about the blood. Where was the DNA? All markers that made the blood unique were gone. It was still blood, the same as it ever was, but only to the naked eye. Once you delved in deeper, got inside, it was blank.

It gave her a chill thinking about it. It wasn't right. She'd thought the sample was contaminated at first, but then they'd checked out Clarke's car, and the bloody snow behind the Carey house. All the same. Lots of blood and nothing else. Where were the bodies? They couldn't be alive, not with that much blood loss. In fact, in the case of the Carey man and boy, she was pretty sure she'd seen more than two people's worth of blood. Were there other bodies out there? Other missing persons who hadn't been reported yet?

She sipped her coffee, trying to make the breakfast last. It wasn't anything special—eggs, sausage links, wheat toast—but it tasted reasonably good. She set her head in her hands and let her eyes close. Sleep tugged at her. She couldn't drive all the way down to Portland feeling like this. She let one eye open. With the volume of snow out there, she wouldn't need to. She could go back to her room and see what was on TV, she guessed. At least she was getting paid.

The waitress appeared at her table. The girl looked like hell. "More coffee?" She didn't even try to smile.

Lee did smile, and the waitress seemed to appreciate it.

"No thanks. When do they expect this storm will wrap up?"

The girl peered out the window. "Tomorrow morning, I think. It's going to be a doozie."

Just what she fucking needed. Though if she were snowed in here, Vince was too. If there weren't any more incidents, maybe they'd be snowed in together. She let her mind roll over the possibility of a day in a motel room with Vince, curled up in bed as snow fell outside. Let it snow, let it snow, let it snow.

A couple came in and ordered breakfast. After all the drama of the morning, Lee braced herself for more confrontation, shunning the waitress, but they were pleasant.

Outside the snow fell and fell, in big, fluffy clumps. It fell so fast, so hard. White blanketed everything outside the window. It felt like dusk though it wasn't even nine in the morning. Looking out there made Lee feel cold and she rubbed at her arms.

The hot cook came out and took a seat at the bar.

"Hey." He turned in response. "Anything interesting to do around here?"

He looked out the window. "Not a damn thing. You a cop?"

"No. I'm a forensic analyst."

"I guess we do have our share of forensics to analyze right about now."

"Not enough. I wish I'd get called in."

"Phones don't work up here."

"I have a radio. Nothing fun to do? Nothing at all?"

"Drinking, screwing, and smoking. Since you work with the cops, I bet you're not going to do any of the above."

If Vince were here, she'd happily be doing at least one of them. She should check on him. Or should she not...? Did that seem needy? The weather was shit, after all. Really awful out there. Her showing interest in his whereabouts during a blizzard wouldn't be a flashing red signal to people saying they were sleeping together.

She smiled at Jason. "Can you refill my coffee? I'm going to step out for a moment."

"Sure thing. You'll need it, it's fucking cold out there. Minus ten and falling."

"I thought it couldn't snow when it was that cold."

"I used to think so too. Rocky Rhodes has proven me wrong."

He smiled at her and she pulled on her coat, gloves and a hat. She slung her bag over her shoulder, even though she knew it would be perfectly safe there in the booth.

Outside, all was silence. Big, heavy snowflakes pelted her. It looked like it had been a while since a plow had passed, a single row of tire tracks in the road rapidly filled with snow. Nothing moved, and with the diner at her back, she could imagine there was nothing left in the whole world. Only her and the snow.

Her nose hairs were freezing. God, she hated this. She had to pull her glove off with her teeth to work the radio. She tried Vince directly, but received only a low static for her trouble. It sounded impossibly loud in the quiet, and she shut it off. She didn't want to be disturbing any...*thing*. There wasn't an anyone out here to bother.

She tried Dispatch next. She radioed in and counted slowly to five before a tired-sounding man answered.

"This is Forensic Analyst LeeAnne Dudley. I'm looking for a twenty on Officer Staghorn."

"We last hear from Staghorn responding to a disturbance on River Road in Rocky Rhodes. Have tried to reach him, he is not responding."

Ice—the metaphysical kind, not the kind all around her—sluiced down her back.

"Have you sent backup?"

"Honey, look around out here. We don't have backup this morning. Everyone's at full tilt." She grit her teeth. She hated, hated, *hated* being called honey. This wasn't the South, and most of the time people did it to be dismissive.

"When did you last hear from him?"

"About thirty minutes ago."

He'd only been gone forty. So he left, radioed in, and hadn't been heard from since?

The second victim died on River Road.

"Thank you, Dispatch."

Lee headed back into the diner, stomping snow off. She slid back in the booth to think over the steaming cup of coffee. She sipped at it while she let her mind work.

She had to go after him, obviously. He'd clearly gone off the road, clearly couldn't get to his radio.

Unless he met the killer.

She tried to will the thought away. Without a body, Staghorn and the other cops said they couldn't call it a killer, that the deceased were technically still missing persons. Lee saw those blood pools. None of the missing would have enough blood in them to survive after an exsanguinating incident like those. Unless the blood wasn't all theirs, which she supposed was possible. A chemical reaction had stripped down the blood, removed any unique identifiers, making it a generic, useless substance. The red and white cells had been scrubbed of anything useful, and remained lifeless husks.

The coffee burned her mouth, and her icy fingers almost couldn't hold the mug. She pulled the state credit card from her purse, and took the coffee to the counter.

"Where are you going?" the cute cook asked. The waitress

stood with the other couple in the diner. She laughed at something the man said. Good to see her smiling.

"No one's heard from the trooper I came in with. I'm going
to find him."

He studied her.

"What are you driving?"

None of his fucking business, that's what she was driving.
"I'm fine, thanks." She thrust the card at him.

"It's the RV, right? You can't take that out in shit like this.
There's likely trees down in the road, and you wouldn't be able
to turn it around to get out."

"I can handle the RV."

"You a good driver?" he asked.

She glared at him. He wasn't so cute anymore. He needed
to take her money so she could get out of here. He didn't take
the card.

"Are you a good driver?"

"I guess."

"I guess, or yes? You from here? Been driving in snow all
your life?"

She scoffed at him. "I'm not from here. I grew up—and
learned to drive—in Wyoming. We had a lot more snow out
there than here. So yes, I'm a good driver in the snow."

He took her card, rang up her breakfast.

"You drive stick?"

"Is this twenty questions?"

"Yeah, it is."

"I can drive stick." Her personal car was a stick, a Subaru.
She preferred it.

He gave her the credit card back along with a set of keys.
"Take my Jeep."

"Sir, I'm not taking your Jeep."

"Jason. There's a CB in it so you can radio if you run into
trouble."

"Jason, I'm not taking your Jeep."

"There's something out there. I'm worried about your
friend."

"He's a trooper. He's fine."

"Why hasn't he radioed in yet?"

She knew Jason was right. She stared at the keys on the counter, and weighed the pros and cons. She hadn't been excited to drive the RV in the snow, and a four-wheel drive Jeep would be great. But taking a stranger's car in a blizzard? She wasn't entirely comfortable with that. She stalked to the window and looked out. A station wagon inched down the main street, its hazards blinking. She turned back and scrutinized Jason's face. He seemed well-meaning. She took the keys. Their fingers brushed, but at that moment, Jason turned to check on the waitress. She laughed again, having sat down with the couple.

"Gassed up?"

"Yes, ma'am."

"Lee."

He held out a hand and they shook on it.

"It's parked around back. Use the four-wheel drive, it's got big old studded tires. It's a powerhouse in snow like this."

"Thank you."

"Make sure it comes back."

"Will do."

She took her card back and finished the still-scalding coffee. She'd pay for it later with a burn on the roof of her mouth, but she relished the warmth in her core.

14 – BURLEIGH

Nate sat with Burleigh in Burleigh's jacked-up Subaru, passing the joint back and forth. Nate had been going strong on the abortion topic for a while, but his weed was good, so Burleigh tried to focus on the floaty feeling of the high, and on the pretty blue-white smoke curling from the tip of the joint.

Wind and snow buffeted the car. He left the engine running, wipers on, defrost on max, but ice still crept in around the top of the windshield. He stared out into the afternoon light. Snow falling and falling and falling. It drew Burleigh in; he could get lost in it.

Nate said something about how Angela had taken a piece of his heart that day.

"Dude," Burleigh finally said. "You, like, don't even want kids."

"I never said that. I wasn't ready before. And besides, Ange would take care of them. I'd make the money, work all day."

Burleigh wanted to say he didn't think it worked like that these days, but he kept his trap shut.

"We're getting back together," Nate said.

This news surprised Burleigh. He'd heard Angela moved back with her dad, and hoped to get out of Dodge ASAP.

"I have a plan." Nate sucked on the joint. "I know how to get her back."

When he passed it back to Burleigh, the tip was wet and mushy. Gross. It was almost gone anyway.

"You gonna do flowers?"

"Something like that. It's like training a dog, you know? Positive and negative reinforcement. Right now we're in the negative reinforcement stage."

Burleigh wanted to suggest that simply being with Nate must be pretty negative, but he wasn't so high not to know to keep quiet. He wanted to giggle, but stared at the dirty floor until it passed.

"What?" Nate asked.

Burleigh gave him a *Who, me?* look.

"You're smiling."

He pointed at a sticker on his dashboard of Scrappy Doo. "Little fucker cracks me up every time."

Nate rolled his eyes. "I gotta run. You can keep the rest. Maybe next week we can get together with the girls? Go out to dinner in Greenville with Sue and Ange?"

"Maybe." Sue made it clear she wouldn't piss on Nate if he were on fire. And she said she felt Angela was too much of a lost cause. "I'll check with her, see what she's got going on."

Nate got out, went over to his Explorer, parked next to the Subaru. Burleigh smoked and listened to Nate scraping. He kept thinking he should go help, but the falling flakes kept his attention. He didn't notice when Nate drove away.

He knew he needed to go check his trap line. He trapped for beaver and raccoon, and could usually sell the pelts to some of the touristy places in Millinocket or Greenville. He should have been out here last night, before the snow hit, but Sue wanted him to come and have dinner with her and her folks. He'd rather have been out here in the cold. The snow fell like crazy now, and it would be getting dark soon. There probably wouldn't be much out there in the storm, but if some critter had been dumb enough to get itself stuck, he didn't want to lose the pelt if something bigger came along and made a snack of it. Fisher cats were usually too smart to get caught, but seemed to know just when to treat the small trap line like a buffet. Burleigh took a final pull off the joint and felt his head swim. Killer weed. He sucked it till his fingers burned. He deposited the end in the Subaru's ashtray. Then he pulled on his hat and gloves, killed the engine, and went out into the storm.

The wind that shook the car made it hard to walk standing straight, so he bent at the waist and leaned into the wind. It was better in the forest, where the canopy and branches protected him. He followed marks on the trees to his trap line. The first one was empty, the bait still in place. It was a good sign, because the fishers were good at yanking bait off without tripping the body-gripping traps. How they did it, he'd never know.

He liked being out here. Made him think of his grandfather, who'd worked this land in the same way from the time he was eight until the accident at the paper mill. Burleigh's feet were warm in his heavy boots, and the pot made him feel like the world was made of cotton candy. He started to whistle, but the woods were too quiet. He shut up and enjoyed the solitude.

At the third trap he found a raccoon, still and covered in snow. He took a few moments to work the trap free, tucked the carcass into his bag, and reset the trap. It was a nice-looking catch, about twenty pounds, and the pelt glossy and neat. Some tourist would be wearing it as a hat. The next two traps were depressingly empty, and his last one showed some tufts of fur. Something'd had a near miss. One fucking raccoon? What a waste of time.

He heard something in the snow and studied the forest. Nothing out of the ordinary. Just another storm in this winter of storms. They'd broken the snowfall record for the month in the first week, and one more dump after this one and they'd be breathing down the record for the whole winter.

Burleigh readjusted his bag and stopped to look at a weird scrape mark on a pine trunk. He'd never seen anything like it. The bark was pulled off, but it didn't seem to be from claws. He leaned in to examine it, when he heard a noise in the forest behind him.

He turned, expecting one of those fucking fisher cats. Sue thought they were cute, but she didn't appreciate how nasty— All thoughts of Sue scattered from his brain. He let the sack with the raccoon drop to the snow.

A woman stood in the woods. Beautiful. Holy fuck was he horny. And the way she smiled at him, she was too. She waved. Smiled at him. Beckoned him. How could he say no to that? Her white dress blended in with the snow. It wasn't even cold anymore out here.

He started talking to her. Babbling. "I'm Burleigh Lewis. Out checking my traps. I got a raccoon, a pretty good one."

She kissed him. Electricity shot though every fiber of his being. She was amazing. He imagined their lives together, flashing ahead of him. He pressed his body into hers and she was perfect, fitting to him, wrapping her arms around him, filling him and completing him. His heart sang and every pleasure receptor on his body cried out. He was so lucky. Lucky he found her, lucky she loved him as much as he loved her. Her love filled him, flowing to every nook and cranny in him, colonizing with her amazingness.

Burleigh Lewis didn't notice when the sharp spine inserted itself in his back, sliding between the vertebrae. By the time he died, exploding into a spattering of blood, his mind had moved on to a happy, wonderful place.

15 – LEE

It took Lee a few blocks to get the hang of the Jeep's transmission, but by the time she drove out of the tiny town and into the woods, she's stopped grinding the gears and swerving all over the road. She had to find Vince. She pushed Jason's Jeep harder, coaxing it around a snowy corner. The gray of the day blended with the white of the landscape, rendering everything gloomy and miserable. Trees, old-growth forest, bare of leaves, crowded the road. She tried to remind herself of all the perfectly plausible reasons why Vince might not have checked in. The storm knocking out the radio tower. Him stuck in a ditch somewhere, waiting for her to save him. Plenty of good reasons they would laugh about later.

She looked at the swirling snow. The Jeep's windshield wipers shot back and forth at maximum velocity, and could barely hold back the falling white. The inside of the windshield started to fog up, so she cranked the heat to defrost. Worst of all, the Jeep had a thermometer on its dash, and it read -10. Living in Wyoming, then Minnesota, then Maine, she wasn't a stranger to these temperatures. Every so often, though, she would ask herself what the *fuck* she was doing in a place like this and not Miami or San Diego.

She allowed herself to imagine taking Vince and going someplace warm, leaving everything here behind her.

She wouldn't want that, no matter how much she thought she did. He was too set in his ways, too conservative. And she didn't really like kids all that much.

Whenever she started thinking about the realities of her relationship with him, she forced it away and reminded herself of the good sex, how when he looked at her, she felt like a high school girl again, felt so desired.

Lee drove for two hours, thinking, worrying, and scanning the side of the road for any sign of Vince. She radioed Dispatch a few times, but they didn't have any new information for her. It was a big county, they said, and they'd send someone to check it out as soon as they could spare the manpower. She hardly saw another person on the road. A few four-wheel-drive vehicles braved the storm, a few snowmobiles, and a few bundled people on foot. Mostly smoke curled from chimneys and candlelight burned in windows. People stayed hunkered down. When the gas in the tank hovered near half, she decided to call it a day and head back to the diner. At least she hadn't totaled Jason's Jeep. She hit a patch of ice and fishtailed. Cool panic washed over her, and she dedicated all her thoughts to keeping the vehicle on the road. She slowed down. That was what happened when she thought about totaling the Jeep. The rest of the way to the diner passed without incident.

She parked out back, behind the diner, and banged on the back door. Jason opened it. His gaze darted past her to his vehicle, and gave it a cursory inspection from where he stood.

"She's back to you safe and sound."

"Good thing. I missed her like crazy. Come on in out of the cold."

Lee followed him into the diner, through the kitchen. Only a few people hung out in the dining room, and no one was ordering food. Angela and Jason had been playing cards.

"Did you find him?" Jason asked, taking his seat in the booth across from Angela.

"No. No sign of him. It's pretty awful out there." Lee wondered if she should stay here, or go back to the motel room. She wasn't even going to attempt driving the RV in this weather.

"Do you want us to deal you in?" Angela asked. "We're almost done this game, you can play the next."

Lee wanted to say no. Wanted to go and be alone. But she knew this would be better. If she went off by herself, she knew she would obsess and fixate on Vince. This would take her mind off it. Any number of things could have happened. People survived all sorts of things. Vince would be fine. Maybe a little frostbitten, but fine. She pulled a chair to the edge of the table, and sat down.

"If you don't mind, I'd love to play."

16 – ANGELA

Jason asked her a million times if he could give her a ride home, but she told him a million times she'd rather walk. It wasn't like anyone was out in this weather anyway. Angela put on her scarf, her coat, her hat, and her mittens, aware of Jason watching her the whole time.

"Can you do me a favor?" he asked.

"A favor? Me?"

"Yeah. Call me when you get home."

She imagined explaining that to her father. "No, Jason. I'm a big girl. I'll be fine."

"It's really crappy out there, and people spray-painted your house last night."

"I'm fine. I promise."

She left him, feeling like she'd let him down. She didn't want to lead him on. Didn't want to tell her father why she was calling him, and what if he wanted to talk? They only had the one phone in the kitchen.

Back in high school, she would sit with her back against the counter, wrapping the cord around her fingers, talking to Nate for hours.

She missed him. She let herself admit it there in the icy wind and swirling snow. Jason would crucify her if he knew, and she'd been squishing it down all day. But she missed him. And now she had the dual drama of missing him *and* hating herself for missing him.

About halfway to her house, she started to regret not taking Jason up on his offer. She'd ridden in his Jeep before. He kept it clean and it smelled like leather and Old Spice. Nate's Explorer, in contrast, always smelled like smoke and rotting food and the garbage on the floor reached her ankles.

She saw headlights turning out of her road, and for a moment they blinded her. Cool blues, so bright they hurt. *Oh no.* She'd done this to herself, brought it upon herself by missing him. She objectively knew he was awful, knew she oughtn't talk to him. And here he was.

He pulled up beside her, the big SUV rumbling.

"Get in the car."

His voice was tight, pinched, and his breath smelled like the cinnamon gum he always chewed. Big Red.

"I'm all right, thanks."

"I didn't ask."

"I don't need a ride. I'm almost home."

"I'm not giving you a ride. Get in the car."

She looked at him for the first time now. There he was, and his bare hand held a handgun out the window, pointed at her. It gave her an excuse to go. She told herself she wouldn't have gone otherwise, she would have run home. But he had a gun.

She trudged through the snow around to the passenger side. She got in, and buckled her seat belt.

Nate drove her to his place. To the apartment she still couldn't help but think of as home. He pointed the gun at her as he moved around the car to let her out, as he forced her up the outdoor stairs to the second-floor apartment. She opened the door. It wasn't locked. No one around here ever locked anything.

A wave of stink assaulted her. Trash spilled out of the car, the sink was heaped with dishes. It was cold in the apartment. The heat and the electric were both out.

"Look at this," he whispered. "Look at what I am without you."

He used the gun to sit her on the couch. He sat beside her, keeping a respectful distance.

"I don't want to pressure you. I know you need time. I've looked at all the studies, and abortion is really tightly linked with depression. You've probably started to realize what it is you've done, and the regret has started to sink in."

Nate was right, but he wasn't. Of course she regretted it. But then she looked around. She couldn't have brought a baby here, not even when she used to keep the place spotless.

"We'll take time. We'll get back to where we were. I need a hug."

"No." She barely spoke above a whisper, but the apartment was quiet. His eyes flashed. He didn't like it when she said no to him.

"Ange, come on. I'm trying to work with you."

"No, you're not. You kidnapped me off the street at gunpoint." Holy cow, she'd never spoken to him like that.

"Kidnapped you? Please." He brought the gun up to her temple. Bonked it against her, hard. It smarted. "Give me a hug."

"Nate, let me go home."

He tapped the gun against her forehead again in the same spot. It really hurt. Was going to leave a bruise. He held his left arm out, welcoming her in for a hug. She held out a moment longer.

"I don't have to shoot you to make you regret not listening to me."

He was right, of course. He knew where to hit, right where to not leave bruises. The thing was, she *wanted* to be with him. She hadn't wanted to leave him, but he was so awful she didn't have a choice. If he could just…not be so awful to her. If he could just be nice… Why couldn't he be nice?

The word almost didn't come out, but she forced it, terrified of the consequences.

"No."

"I don't think I heard you."

"I said no." It came easier the second time. She folded her hands in her lap so he wouldn't see they were shaking.

He studied her, and she wondered what anyone would do if he killed her. They'd all say they'd seen it coming. He lashed out fast and she suspected he meant to hit her in the kidney, but she moved enough so he got her in the ribs. She flopped back on the couch, clutching where it hurt.

"Come here."

She didn't want him to hit her again.

She went to him and rested her head on his shoulder. He

stank, he needed to take a shower. Whatever, she smelled like fryer grease. "I'm not doing this because I want to," she said. It was stupid to have missed him.

He slapped her face, not hard enough to even leave a red mark. Then he set the gun on the coffee table, and wrapped his arms around her. He told her she was beautiful, and he loved her so much. He'd missed her.

"We're going to take this really slow, baby. You'll see your place is here with me."

"You can't hold a gun on me all the time."

"And I don't need to." He pulled back and looked at her face. Tucked a strand of hair behind her ear. "We're okay, baby. We'll make this work."

He leaned in for a kiss and she braced herself, but he only kissed her cheek.

"You're going to need to get some beauty sleep."

Okay, she could wait for him to fall asleep, and sneak out the window. It was cold, and snowing, and she wouldn't have her coat or anything, but she could make it to the church or maybe even home to her dad's house. Nate was a heavy sleeper, and once he was out, she'd be home free.

"I'm going to show you what a gentleman I am," he told her. It made her skin crawl. "You may have the bedroom, and I will sleep on the couch." He'd never slept on the couch. Not once in two years. He got mad at her if she tried to, didn't matter if she couldn't sleep, he had a hacking cough, they'd had a fight, or what. They slept together.

This was better. She could slip out the window easily, there was a fire escape right outside. She'd give it a half hour, and she'd be gone. She relaxed a bit.

Nate rubbed her back. "My girl looks tired. Let's get you into bed."

He left the gun behind, which was good, but he walked her with his hands on her shoulders. She couldn't get away if she wanted to.

The bed was made, and the sheets smelled clean as she turned the blankets down.

"I get it if you don't want to undress in front of me right now.

We've been through a lot. But in a few weeks, I promise we'll look back on this and wonder what the fuck you were thinking when you left me and aborted my fucking son." Anger and malice slipped into his voice.

He kissed her on the mouth this time, running his fingers through her hair. He didn't open his mouth, didn't try to grope her or anything.

"Sleep well, beautiful. I'll see you in the morning."

He left her sitting on the bed, and headed for the door. "Oh, if you have to take a piss, I left you a bucket in the corner. Just don't knock it over. It'd be hard to get out of the carpet."

He closed the door and she heard the snap of a lock. She flew to the window, pulled the heavy curtains aside, and found bars over the window. Her heart plummeted. And worse, she had to pee. *He'd planned this.* The realization chilled her as she looked at the plain tan bucket in the corner.

Was this better than if she'd stayed put and had the baby? Who was she to think she could get out? She crumpled onto the bed, tucking her head under her arms.

17 – LEE

Lee spent most of the afternoon curled in one of the diner booths reading. Worry gnawed at her, but there were a lot of good reasons why Vince may not have checked in. Maybe a kind person gave him shelter from the storm and he sat tucked in near a fire while the storm covered his patrol car outside. She pushed aside the other explanations that left him dead and freezing on the side of the road. He was a good driver. In the awful weather he wouldn't have driven at speeds that could get him killed.

She didn't get a lot of reading done.

Jason made hamburgers for an early dinner, bragging that even if the power and the genny went out, the propane grill wouldn't leave them hungry.

After dark, Jason decided to close up the diner. He'd argued with Angela about letting him give her a ride home. They all needed to leave that poor girl alone. Someone was always up her ass for something. Lee silently cheered when Angela told him no, she would not call him when she got home.

Lee hung around as he closed the place down. He'd already offered to drive her back to the motel. She wasn't going to try to move the RV until the storm ended and the plow trucks started making more than their feeble token passes. She was tired with a listless exhaustion, having done nothing all day but stare out the window and worry about the storm. What was the weather like down in Portland? Without a TV or radio, the Internet or any other goddamn means of communication, she couldn't know. Could be snowing there, or it could have completely fallen off the planet. There may not even be anything left in the world except Rocky Rhodes, snow, and weird, tainted blood...

"Ready?" Jason finally asked. He pulled on a coat, a hat, and gloves. Lee did the same. It would feel good to get out of these boots. Fuck this place so hard.

She followed him out where she'd parked the Jeep and they spent a long while not talking and digging it out of the snow. By the time they got inside, the cab was toasty warm.

"You at the Cedar Pines?"

"Is there another motel in town?" What was it, the *Birch Maple*?

"A B&B on the outskirts. Almost heading to Greenville."

"Nope, I'm at the Cedar Pines. Who runs that place? Do they get how trees work? Cedars are not pines."

Jason chuckled. He drove slowly, the Jeep's big tires struggling in the snow. A prickle of dread blossomed in Lee. She didn't want to go back to the motel. Didn't want to see Vince's closed door, know his stuff was in there, waiting for him to come back.

"Listen." She didn't know how to say this, so she spat it out. "Can I stay with you tonight? I'm not really wild about the idea of being alone. If you've got something else going on, that's totally fine, I'm cool being alone. Nothing bad will happen if I'm, I just—"

"I would love your company," he said.

She wanted to tell him she'd sleep on the couch, no funny business. She wanted companionship. But she didn't, because she was curious where the night would take them. She was pretty sure he was so tangled up with Angela he wouldn't try anything. It made her feel a little dirty.

"I'll take the couch, and you can crash in my bed."

"I don't want to turn you into a displaced person."

"I'm not sure I'm going to get much sleep."

"Worried about Angela?"

"Yeah. I know it's dumb. I'm sure it's dumb."

"She'll be fine. She probably needed some time alone. I should have given her my motel room."

"Her dad's rough to be around. Super strict. She went right from him to Nate. God, I hate that guy."

Jason pulled up in front of a small ranch house. "Home sweet home." The house was dark, and so were the streetlights around it. "I'll get a fire going, and we'll be warm in no time."

The house gave the impression of a temporary lodging, nothing on the walls. The mismatched furniture looked like it came from thrift stores. The couch was comfortable, and he kept a clean house. He pulled out some LED lanterns. They threw off a sterile blue glow. Jason built a fire, and soon it was warm enough to take off their coats. She watched the flames of the fire while Jason checked to see if any pipes had frozen while the power was out.

"We don't have tornadoes, don't have earthquakes, don't have wildfires. Snow's not so bad when you think about it."

If it wasn't so bad, where was Vince? They should have been hunkered down together in the Cedar Pines Motel. Instead she sat here with a stranger. "You're right," she told him. She tried radioing dispatch one final time before turning in, and they snapped at her to keep the lines clear.

"He's missing," she told Jason.

"You'll find him tomorrow."

She shyly asked him to share the bed with her, and he agreed, but he spent the night as a perfect gentleman, and barely brushed against her in the night. He didn't snore.

18 - Mary Beth

A strange banging echoed outside. Or was it her hangover, her headache? Mary Beth couldn't tell. Every day when she woke up now, it was all the same. Dennis was gone.

Another sound reached her and first she wasn't sure what it was, then realized it was a wailing. Oh God, was it she? No, her mouth was closed. It so wouldn't have surprised her to find she'd been crying. The TV? She pulled herself out of the cocoon of her blankets, taking the afghan her gran made her and wrapping it around her shoulders. She went to the living room.

Snowing again? Really? Already? Each year she hated this weather more and more. She didn't ski, didn't snowboard, none of that bullshit. She didn't like ice fishing or snowmobiles, snowshoeing or ice climbing. All winter was, for her, a pain in the ass. She dreamed about moving someplace warm. Dennis liked it here. Had she been staying for him?

Maybe next winter it would be time to head south.

She'd fallen asleep sometime yesterday, and she couldn't see a clock, but she knew she'd slept a long time. Maybe around the clock. It was dark out, which meant it could be four in the afternoon, or four in the morning. She felt dehydrated and disoriented.

That sound again. There it was. She didn't like it. Didn't like it at all.

She looked around and didn't know where it came from. She shook her head to clear the sleep out. She looked at the clock on the cable box, but it sat dark. The power was out? Goddammit.

Nate?

Ice crept down her spine. It couldn't be Nate. She wouldn't

let that happen. Everything was dark outside; she didn't want to draw attention to herself by pulling the curtains back.

It sounded like a ghost from a kids' haunted house, an "ooooOOOOooo" sound. Someone fucking with her? Almost definitely Nate. She couldn't imagine what he wanted from her, why he would come back. He had all those chicks, all over him, all the time. Why her? She'd never been particularly cool or uncool—drugs kept her on pretty good terms with the "popular kids" in school. If someone picked on her, she told them she didn't have any weed for a few weeks, and they'd come around. She knew she bought her friends, but a heavy girl didn't have too many other choices. She took what she could get. But Nate? Girls had been hanging off him since they heard him and Angela had broken up. They'd mobbed him, swarmed him. So why was he here, pretending to be a ghost?

She heard the sound again, this time punctuated with a trembling sob at the end. She pulled back the towel nailed over the window, a makeshift curtain.

Snow. Big, fat, fluffy flakes, hurling down from the sky. The beginning of Winter Storm Zeus, as The Weather Channel called it—they named winter storms now, too. The last was Winter Storm Xcalibur, and had amounted to a dusting up here in Maine. Boston had gotten some snow, but not enough to warrant a name. At least not a name like Xcalibur. Maybe Winter Storm Leopold or Winter Storm Poindexter. Something dorky.

From where she peeked out the window, she couldn't see anything; the snow in the driveway sparkled undisturbed before her. Like crystallized sugar on a white frosted cookie. Nate wouldn't come on foot, on snowshoes. He would have come in his stupid truck. So it wasn't Nate.

"OoooOOOOooooo!" Followed up by a sob.

From the living room window, she couldn't see the stairs leading up to the little entryway where the sound came from. Someone at the door? Some*thing* at the door?

Something pounded. Snow fell off the entryway roof.

Mary Beth watched a lot of horror movies. Dennis liked them—*had* liked them—and she thought some of them were pretty cool. Sometimes she got spooked out here alone.

Sometimes she wished for a dog or a gun to keep her company.

Thump.

Sweating now, she dropped the blanket. In the kitchen, she grabbed a big old cast-iron frying pan, so heavy she held it in both hands. Would this really work against an assailant?

The word *assailant* made it worse.

Maybe the door was open, and the hinge was...what, sobbing in the wind?

Thump thump thump!

A muffled voice "Please!"

Someone was out there. Her power was out, so the only phone was the one on the wall. She'd seen the horror movies. She was going to call 911 before she thought about opening the door.

A little voice spoke in the back of her mind. *The phone lines are down too.* The power is out.

They'd buried the phone lines a few years back. They figured since there was no cell signal and the power went out every other week or so in the winter, there had to be something reliable so people wouldn't be stranded all alone, unable to call 911.

Mary Beth held her breath and picked up the line.

A dial tone greeted her. Relief washed over her, flooded her, weakened her knees.

She punched those three numbers, which she hadn't done since she and her best friend in sixth grade dared each other to call and hang up.

"This is 911, can I help you?"

Fifteen years ago, she and Jada looked at each other in horror, and slammed the line down.

"This is Mary Beth Stanton. There's someone outside my house. They say they need help. Should I let them in?"

The operator was from Millinocket, dispatching to all the rural communities. If dispatch had been Rocky Rhodes, they could have sent someone without asking where she lived. Everyone knew where Mary Beth lived. She gave her address.

"I'm going to go to the door."

The operator agreed to wait on the line. A car was coming,

she said. An officer was patrolling north of Rocky Rhodes; he would be there very soon.

Not soon enough.

She set the phone down, careful not to clunk it in the operator's ear. She steadied herself with a deep breath, then another.

Again the cry came. "Please. Help me!"

Mary Beth went to the door.

When she pulled it open, a shaking form, blue from the cold, spilled in. Snow swirled around it, had piled up on the person's shoulders and head.

"Can you stand?" she asked.

It was a trap. Had to be. The person would spring up, and stick a knife in her back. He'd be gone long before the cops ever showed up.

The form made a weak noise. Mary Beth reached down and hauled the person into her kitchen, by the woodstove. She picked up her blanket, and wrapped it around its shoulders. She brushed snow off the face.

A woman. That made her feel better.

The woman clutched at the blanket, wrapped it closer around herself. She shook and her teeth chattered; her lips a horrid shade of blue. Her cheeks were gray—frostbite. She wore big hoop earrings, and lots of studs in each ear. She definitely wasn't from around here.

"What's your name? What happened to you?"

Mary Beth went back to the door to close up. She knew to stay on the right side of it, more than once it had blown shut and locked her out. Not a problem when the windows were open in the summer. She didn't want to deal with it today. The girl had come from the woods, left a weak trail in the snow, which already filled with Zeus's wrath. God, it was really coming down. Could they even get a cop car here? An ambulance?

The girl didn't answer, so Mary Beth went back to the phone. "It's a girl. She's got hypothermia. Shock. I don't know. She's super out of it. Her lips are blue. I've got her near the fire."

Dispatch said they'd see about an ambulance, but she wasn't sure. The cop might have to take her in his car. She advised getting a hot drink for the girl. Mary Beth made a cup of tea from the pot of water she kept on the woodstove.

The girl couldn't take the cup at first.

"What happened?" Mary Beth asked again. She wondered if this had anything to do with the missing Careys. With Dennis. The thought stabbed at her. It hurt.

"There's something in the woods." The girl sounded like she'd smoked a pack and a half of Marlboros. Or her larynx had frozen and was only now thawing.

"What do you mean, *something*?"

"A monster."

"What?"

She started to cry, sloshing scalding-hot tea onto herself. She didn't even react.

A monster. A monster killed Dennis? Impossible, he'd been in his car. How would a monster get inside?

"He's dead," the girl said, in between her tears.

Dennis? Someone else?

An immediate sense of kinship flooded over her. This girl knew what it was like. Knew what she was going through. Might be the only person who could understand.

And she'd seen something out there.

"It likes the cold," she whispered. "Needs it."

Mary Beth shivered. Monsters. Dennis would have liked that.

"The police are coming," she said.

"They'll never believe me."

She was right. It took another hour before the cruiser arrived, sirens on, lights flashing, but only going about five miles an hour down her snowy drive. She would be lucky if they didn't get stuck here. Shit, that was all she needed, a Greenville cop in her driveway for the night. Would they all have a slumber party?

The officer was a young man. When did cops start getting younger than Mary Beth? Weird. He explained there was no ambulance, and a plow truck was following him down the driveway so he could get the car out.

The girl lay asleep on the couch.

"She's talking about monsters in the woods."

"Awesome," the cop said. "That's what my night needs."

"Do you think it might have to do with"—she wanted to say so much more, but settled on—"the recent disappearances?"

"State cops are all over those cases now. I have nothing to do with that shit."

"Jurisdiction gets pretty confusing up here."

"Jurisdiction nothing. We don't deal in murder."

19 – ANGELA

Angela woke having to pee again. Gray light peeked in around the curtains; it must have been after dawn. She'd woken in the night and voided her bladder in the bucket Nate provided, and now the room smelled like pee. She pulled the covers back—at least they were clean and warm. She hated to admit it, but it had been nice to sleep in her own bed again. She'd slept here every night for the past two years, and the queen was much more comfortable than the twin at her dad's house.

Frigid air assaulted her. Nate used a small kerosene heater out in the living room, but with the door closed, none of the warmth came through to her. She pulled down her pants and underwear and hovered herself over the bucket. She couldn't cry anymore. There was a certain inevitability to all of this. So long as she remained in Rocky Rhodes, he would have her. If she got free again—*when* she got free again—she would have to leave. Maybe for good this time.

She tapped on the bedroom door, lightly at first, not wanting to disturb him. Her watch told her it was 6:30. Jason would notice she wasn't at work soon. They'd agreed she'd come in at seven, a late start due to the weather.

Screw it. What did it matter if she disturbed him? Him or Mr. Barthes from downstairs. She pulled on her coat and her boots. She had slept in her hat.

She banged on the door with an open palm.

"Nate! Let me out!"

Let Barthes hear *that*.

She heard the springs on the couch creaking, and heard his shuffling gait cross the floor. She heard the blessed click of the lock, and there was Nate, looking scruffy and tousled. She'd woken him up. She gave him a big smile.

"Keep quiet."

"Morning, honey. I have to go to work." She'd kill more flies with honey than with vinegar, and she had to get out of this apartment. She needed to do whatever it took.

"Stinks in here."

"You had me pee in a bucket. What do you expect?"

He grunted. She rushed to the heater, and held her hands out to its warmth.

"Anyway, I have to be at work at seven. Will you drop me?"

He laughed at her. "Baby, you've got me now. You don't need to work."

"We could use the money."

"Listen to me. My mother doesn't work. Your mother never worked. You're not going to be out there all day slaving your ass off, and letting things go to shit around the house. You've seen what happened since you been gone. I have more than enough for you to do here."

Panic threatened her chest. She couldn't stay here. She couldn't be with him. *Think!* "All right. I can quit after I pick up my check. It's payday today." She didn't even have to lie.

Nate reached for her, though, knocking her off balance and almost into the heater. She had to lean in against him, clutch at him, to keep upright. She hated his familiar feel.

"I know what you want, you fucking slut. You want to go see Jason. You started fucking him the minute you left me. No, you'd probably been fucking him for a while."

She kept quiet.

"Admit it," he said. "Tell me you fucked him."

He took her hand, twisted her wrist around. She let out a squeak of pain.

Nate spoke in her ear, hot morning breath against her face. "Tell me how it was."

Never. She would never cheat on anyone. But anger boiled in her, and the tears in her eyes weren't from fear or pain, but from anger. "He was great," she said. "Loving. Considerate."

Her words shocked him, and she twisted herself away,

darted back, and put the heater between them.

"You're lying."

"You're right. I've still never known a considerate lover."

What are you doing? Don't taunt him. Angela knew never to taunt him. She had to get away now. If she didn't, he might get even more violent.

He lunged at her, and she tipped the space heater into his path, burning her hand in the process.

Hot kerosene poured on Nate's leg and he yowled. She didn't stop. She flipped the lock on the door and bolted, running down the rickety stairs to the little parking area they shared with Mr. Barthes. It was only a half-mile to the diner. That was nothing. She'd had to run much farther distances in gym class.

But so had Nate. Nate played football and worked out. She pushed the thoughts from her mind.

The world was snow. No plows had been out for hours, and the deep drifts made moving hard. She slogged through, looking back every so often. Fate smiled on her and it almost made her dizzy. Sitting on the front porch of the dark house next door. A pair of snowshoes. She waded through waist-high snow, and strapped them to her feet. They changed everything, even though she wasn't really sure how to use them. She tried to run, at first, hearing a car engine behind her. She chanced a peek over her shoulder and saw Nate trying to coax the Explorer free of the snowdrifts.

Angela cut across yards. She left a path, but he stayed in the car, which didn't give him much of an advantage on the unplowed streets. He knew where she was going, though. He had to. Should she go home instead? She crouched under the branches of a pine tree, a temporary respite from the wind and the snow. He couldn't be watching both the front and the back of the diner. She decided to go for the back. When they were together, Nate always brought her to the front, so she hoped that's where he'd be heading now.

She traipsed through the snow toward the diner, but moving her legs seemed to take forever. It wasn't far; she had to be there soon. Behind the diner, her heart sank. Jason's Jeep wasn't there. She looked at her watch, exposing her wrist to the snow. After seven. He had to be there.

Ahead of her gaped an open yard where she could be spotted from the street. She couldn't see any motion out there. None of the diner's windows opened this way, so she couldn't see anything inside.

Awkwardly on the snowshoes, she ran.

If Jason isn't there, there's no one there. She banged on the door anyway, mentally begging the door to open, for him to let her in. In her heart she knew it wouldn't.

She pulled her mitten off and beat on the door with her fist. She shivered and tears ran down her cheeks, freezing there, as she tried to think of her next move. This was all she had. She didn't think she could get from here to her dad's house, not in this weather. In another place she would have had a cell phone, could have called for help.

The door opened.

Jason stood there.

Relief made her knees weak and she almost fell, but he caught her. He pulled her into the warm kitchen. The generator hummed and the lights were on.

"Holy shit, Ange. Are you all right?"

"Nate," she managed. *He kept me for the night. He made me piss in a bucket. He wasn't going to let me go.* She didn't say any of that, though. "He's going to come here."

"I thought I saw him parked out front."

"Where's your Jeep?" Angela unstrapped the snowshoes, and leaned them against the wall by the back door.

"Lee borrowed it, looking for her trooper again."

Jason strode toward the swinging doors, then the dining room. She heard people shouting, someone screamed. A gunshot. Her feet were rooted to the spot.

He was here.

Jason threw open the door. Simultaneously, the gun boomed and Jason fell. The hold on her broke, and she hurled herself forward at Jason. She saw blood, lots of blood, on his face and flowing into his hair. She had to think fast—he'd fallen mostly back into the kitchen. She grabbed him by the shoulders and hauled him backward on the slick floor, rushing to the shelter of a nearby storeroom. She dragged him inside and slammed the door.

Jason had been to war and Jason was paranoid. *Not paranoid enough*, she thought, looking at the prone form on the floor before her. He'd put a mighty lock on the inside of this door, and now she turned it. They were safe in here.

Nate banged on the door. He shouted. He even shot at the lock, but the thick storeroom walls muted the sound. It was elsewhere. She sat on the floor, leaning against a big sack of flour. She set Jason's head in her lap, and she waited.

20 - MARY BETH

Mary Beth saw the cop out to the car, leading the girl, wrapped in an afghan her gran knit. It was okay to lose the afghan. Gran could be a bitch sometimes, but would likely make her another one. She held her keys, nervously jangling them.

"Where are you going to take her?"

"The Greenville station to start, EMMC if we can get her there safely. She looks dehydrated and half-frozen."

The girl didn't seem to mind being talked about as if she weren't there.

Out in the woods came a crashing sound, something huge moving through the trees. It bent them to its will, trunks snapping in its path. Mary Beth jumped, and her keys slipped from her fingers. They landed on the edge of the step, then slid into the darkness separating the house from the trailer.

She looked up at the cop, who didn't look alarmed. The blood drained from her face. Her keys. No way she could get down there to get them.

"What?" the cop asked. "A fucking tree fell."

She shifted her gaze to the woods, and saw he was right. One of the old pines had fallen in the wind.

"I dropped my keys."

He looked at her like she was stupid, and she fought the urge to punch him. She started to shake from the cold. The cop helped the girl in the car, then came up on the step. Together they peered into the small crevasse. Mary Beth, without a coat, held herself and shivered.

The cop dropped to his knees and reached down into the blackness.

Mary Beth monitored the forest. The gray cloud cover of the storm washed everything out with a premature twilight, and the shadows between the trees smudged dark. She glanced down where the keys had fallen. She expected something to reach out, to take hold of his hand, and to pull. Would the arm come off at the shoulder? She imagined white bone, the pink of traumatized, torn muscle, and the crimson blood. How the red splatter would contrast against the fresh white snow.

The cop sat up, still on his knees.

"I can't reach them."

She wasn't even going to try.

"Do you have a stick or something? A magnet?"

In the house. Everything was in the fucking house.

"You think I could get a ride in to town?" she asked.

"To Greenville?"

"Just in to Rocky Rhodes. I got a friend I can stay with."

She couldn't stay here. She thought of her puffy blue Bean jacket hanging inside the door. She'd freeze.

She glanced out at the trees. *Monsters in the woods.*

The girl clearly could have meant human monsters—a lunatic with a gun or a knife.

Except Mary Beth knew she didn't. Dennis would get such a rise out of it. It made her a little bit happy.

"I guess I can drop you. Go on, get in the car."

"Looks like we should go now."

He glared at her, some variation of "you can't tell me my business," but he looked out the window at the blowing sheets of white and nodded.

He opened the back door of the car for her and she balked. The girl already sat up front, huddled in a blanket, staring sightlessly out the front windshield. The backseat was smooth, hard plastic with special grooves so it didn't hurt so bad if your hands were cuffed behind you. Mary Beth had ridden in the back of a police car before. She wasn't keen to do it again. She glanced back at her dark trailer and knew she didn't have too many options. Sherri or Ginger better let her crash at their place. *Unless they're at Nate's.* They couldn't both be at Nate's. She corrected herself. Maybe they *were* both at Nate's. Anything was possible.

She slid into the backseat as she banished the thought from her mind. Through a plastic barrier, she heard the girl's heavy breathing in the front seat. Snow accumulated on the windshield. The car, at least, was warm.

The officer slid behind the wheel. He picked up his radio, but could only get static.

"I hate coming out here," he said to the rearview mirror.

She thought to ask his name, then decided she didn't care.

The tires spun at first, and Mary Beth figured they could break one of the windows in the spare room and climb in that way, but the grip caught and the cruiser lurched forward. The cop fought to gain control. Didn't they have to go through extensive training to be cops? A driving school of some kind?

She stared out the side windows at the white forest. Nothing moved. All the animals were smart enough to hole up, stay hidden. Which is what she'd been doing before the crazy girl up front crashed into her life. She should have stayed in bed.

She couldn't recall the last time she'd seen roads like this. She was glad she wasn't out driving in it. The cop blazed his own trail through piled snow on the roads. He kept trying the radio with no luck.

"Fucking phones don't work out here. Radios don't work. Why do any of you live in this shit hole?"

"Some people like the quiet." She didn't. She'd move. There. Decided. Come spring, or come whenever, she would start looking for a place in Bangor. Someplace with reliable Internet and other people. Other people like her and Dennis, at least.

The cop snorted.

They turned onto River Road. The cop blew through the stop sign, probably worried he'd never get the car going again if he did. It didn't matter, they hadn't seen another car or evidence of another car. In the best of circumstances Rocky Rhodes made it easy to imagine this was the last holdout of humanity. Today it seemed like they were the only ones left alive in the world.

Maybe they were. Maybe those monsters in the snow had already snatched everyone else.

Once on River Road the cop found twin tire tracks to follow, and picked up some speed. On the one hand, it terrified her. On the other hand, she wanted to be out of this fucking car as soon as humanly possible. She chewed on her thumbnail until she tasted salty blood. She kept chewing. The pain felt good.

"What the fuck?" she heard the cop say.

Then they swerved and time slowed down. She rode on a carnival ride, images flashing before her with appalling clarity. Trees, road, trees, road (but back where they'd come from), trees, road, trees…then CRASH! Metal against metal. The impact threw her into the plastic barrier, and she hit her face, she bit her lips and blood gushed from her nose.

The engine died, and the world went silent. From where she'd fallen, all she could see was the ceiling of the car. She did a mental inventory of what hurt and everything felt all right except her banged-up face. Then the car door opened on the driver's side. Cold air and snow whirled in. He left it open.

No, they needed the warmth.

Mary Beth hauled herself up so she could see out the windows.

They'd hit another car that had sat half on, half off the road, at a crazy angle. It was a Maine State Police car, one of the blue ones. The impact tipped it over the embankment, and she knew it was a steep six-foot drop into a frozen creek. She looked around for the trooper, but didn't see him. The girl up front, protected by her seat belt, huddled into her seat.

What she saw next made her breath catch in her throat. She started to cry out, then realized she'd hit her head. What she saw must be a result of powers of suggestion—talk about monsters, poor sleeping. Something. It couldn't be real.

A woman?

No, a *thing* stood in front of the Greenville city cop. If Mary Beth didn't exactly look at it full on, it looked like a woman, but when she studied it, it seemed more like a humanoid blob, poorly formed around the edges.

The girl in the driver's seat saw it, and started to scream. The sound of her screams made Mary Beth's head hurt, explosively loud in the enclosed car.

The thing floated above the snow, moving as though the wind pushed it around. Either that or it drifted to some sonorous music in its own head. It donned a suggestion of a white nightdress, and its legs and arms were bare. The alabaster skin almost didn't stand out from the snow. Hints of long black hair whipped around its face.

The cop didn't seem to care. He moved closer and closer.

"No!" Mary Beth shrieked. The girl in the front flinched. Mary Beth pounded on the window with her palms. So what if this were a dream or a hallucination. She still didn't want to see the cop get...eaten? Splattered? What would happen to him?

Then she looked up.

It was white, so it was almost lost in the snowy branches. She had to stare hard, and like a Magic Eye picture in a book, the image shifted in and out of visibility. It loomed huge over the woman. A two-story worm, thick as a house. Rows upon rows of little legs, and it reared up on its tail.

The cop said something inaudible. She couldn't hear through the thick glass.

He reached out and touched the woman-thing's arm. She turned her dull head to him. Could he be fooled? Up close she must look even less human than she did from back here. Mary Beth pounded on the glass again.

"Now it's going to stick him." The girl in the front's voice was hardly more than a whisper.

Mary Beth turned to the girl, but motion caught her eye.

The monstrosity's tail tapered to a point, and it slashed around, lightning fast. It came at the cop from behind and pierced him in the tailbone, angling upward.

Fluid transferred, but she couldn't tell which way it was going.

This was ridiculous. Couldn't be real. Couldn't possibly be real. She reached out and pinched herself, but the monster was still there, using its tail to pump fluid (*into? Out of?*) a Greenville city cop.

Mary Beth slapped herself. White pain exploded in her vision from her broken nose, but the monster continued to feed.

The girl up front threw open her door and ran out into the winter morning.

"No!"

She left her door open too.

Outside, the cop started to swell, and the white creature's tail took on a pinkish hue.

This happened to Dennis.

She started to cry. She punched at the glass, pushed and kicked and slapped wherever she could think, but she was in the back of a fucking cop car. They designed these things so people bigger and stronger and smarter than she couldn't get out.

Now the creature seemed to be taking more than it gave, and the cop started to fold in on himself. His clothes—the warm department-issued jacket, his fur-lined cap, drew into him as well.

Then?

With a final push of fluid from the monster, the Greenville cop popped. He vaporized, a thick fountain of crimson blood. She understood why she'd never been allowed to see Dennis's car. The realization halted her flowing tears as she stared out the spattered window.

The woman-thing deflated like a blow-up doll, and the monster drew it into one of its folds. It looked larger now. It snuffled the air, a face like a grub, and dropped down onto its stomach and slithered into the forest.

Mary Beth couldn't think. Couldn't cry, couldn't do anything. She stared at the spot where it had vanished. No trail in the snow, unimpeded by trees. This thing couldn't have existed. There was no evidence it had ever been there...except the blood.

Mary Beth wrapped her arms around herself for warmth and curled into the tightest ball she could imagine. She'd wake up soon. Wake up in her bed, and the girl never would have come to her door. Maybe Dennis would be there. They could have at least shut the doors so it would be warmer in here.

She closed her eyes and prayed the cold would take her quickly.

21 – LEE

This time Lee had the subtle nuances of the Jeep and she got a much stronger start. She left in pre-dawn darkness, tired from a mostly sleepless night in a stranger's bed. In retrospect, she was glad he'd been a gentleman. It would have felt cheap and dirty this morning if they'd slept together. She thought about Vince, and pushed away the thought that today she looked for a body. Or a blood splatter.

Something in the road shook her out of her head. She tried to be gentle with the brakes, turning the wheel so she didn't hit the thing, dark in a sea of white. It was too much for the Jeep and it started to wobble. She'd never rolled a vehicle, but she thought she could tell the sensation that would precede it.

She wrestled with the Jeep. How embarrassing to crash a borrowed vehicle. Time slowed as her adrenaline surged and she was back in Wyoming with her father, in a storm with drifts as large as the car. He sat next to her, seat-belted in, telling her to steer into the skid, not to struggle against the vehicle.

Doubtful, she registered the snow banks on one side, the crumpled form—a body—lay in the snowy road. Lee stopped fighting. The Jeep kissed the snow bank and regained its traction, and she eased it to a stop.

She threw open the door and jumped out into the blinding storm. Wind whipped the snow into a fury and it pelted against her. It would tear her skin off, abrade her down to nothing. Outside she started to shiver.

Curled in the snow, hunched where the yellow line would be, lay a woman's body. Lee reached for her shoulder, but found it cold and hard, like cordwood. Her eyes stared sightlessly into the sky, and snow collected in the sockets. Her lips were flat and blue, her cheeks white.

Lee had left the Jeep door open and snow collected on her seat. She brushed it off, and slid inside, holding her gloved hands over the heaters for a moment before picking up the radio to call in the body.

She wasn't even met with static—when she clicked the button on the handset, she heard nothing but dead air. She looked around, hoping to find something to mark this place so she could send someone to collect the corpse. Snowy trees stretched out as far as she could see on either side of the road. They all looked the same.

It didn't take long to freeze to death in these temperatures. All the more reason to move forward and find Vince. The woman was dead, nothing Lee could do would change that. Vince was out there somewhere, he had to be.

She put the Jeep in first and nudged it forward, inching around the body. She drove slower this time, not interested in repeating her earlier loss of traction. Why had the woman been out in the storm? Where was her car? Lee peered at the forest—the car could easily have gone off the road and be buried in a snowdrift, the tracks already vanished from sight. God she hated the snow. Hated how it obliterated everything and turned it smooth and round and sparkling.

The road narrowed, and the turns grew sharper. She slowed the Jeep to a crawl. She had to keep moving up the slight incline. If she stopped, she didn't know if the thing could go again, fat studded tires or no.

She wasn't going fast, but the police car—Greenville police— in the middle of the road made her brake too hard, sending the Jeep's ass end into a fishtail. She caught some ice and the Jeep launched into a slow-speed skid, finally coming to a rest as it thudded into the police car. The impact closed the open passenger door. She couldn't open her door, it was pressed against the cruiser's right side. She peeked out her window and saw a huddled form in the back of the other car.

Lee wasn't a stranger to death or to bodies. When the cases were easy, they brought the evidence to her in the lab. When the cases were challenging, they called her out to the field. She'd seen things she wished she could forget.

The body in the cruiser was another woman, a bigger lady, curled into a tight ball, knees to her chest, arms wrapped around them for warmth. A helpless rage swam up inside Lee. She couldn't do anything for these two. How many more would she see today?

In the warm cabin of the Jeep, Lee let herself cry. Normally she didn't, but there wasn't anyone here to judge her other than the forlorn body in the back of the cruiser. Who was she, and why had she been arrested? She wasn't cuffed, which seemed odd.

More importantly, where was the officer? The driver's door hung open, and in the howling wind she could hear the "bing, bing, bing" indicating the keys were still in the ignition and the battery had yet to run down.

Jesus, where was the officer?

She pulled the Jeep into reverse and scraped herself along the cruiser. The Jeep was game, and let itself be pulled free.

The slightest motion, so tiny she thought she was imagining things, came from the back of the police car. She parked the Jeep, flipped on the hazards and stepped out into the storm, scanning the woods and the area for a sign of the officer. She opened the back door to the car.

The woman lifted her head.

"You're real?" she mumbled.

"You're alive!"

Lee reached in and started to haul the woman off the slick plastic backseat of the cruiser. She was heavy, and her arms felt so cold, even compared to the screaming winter outside. Lee opened the Jeep's door and helped the woman into the warmth.

"Where's the officer?" she asked.

In the warmth, the woman started to shiver. Lee got inside and closed her door. She wanted to minimize the amount of air spilling from the vehicle.

"What's your name? I'm Lee."

The woman's chattering teeth made her hard to understand. "Did it kill Jason?"

It took Lee a moment to process what she'd said, rolling it around in her mind. "No! He's back at the diner. He let me drive his Jeep out here because it's better in the snow."

She looked relieved to hear Jason was safe.

"Mary Beth," the woman said.

"What?"

"My name is Mary Beth."

"Where's the officer?"

"He hit the trooper's car. He's dead. The trooper's car went off the road right there." Mary Beth pointed with a shaking hand to the far side of the car. Lee saw a faint depression in the snow on the side of the road.

Trooper's car. Off the road. Lee flung herself out of the Jeep, leaving it running. She made her way around the car, slipping once and having to catch herself on the trunk. There were a lot of troopers in the state of Maine, and probably Vince couldn't be the only one up here. This was a strange case, it only made sense he'd have some backup.

The blue Crown Vic sat at an odd angle, one of the wheels completely up and out of the snow. It was almost buried, the trunk submerged in fluffy white, but the wind kept the windshield and hood blown clean. She couldn't see inside. Blood and gore spattered the interior of the windows.

The car was his.

Just because there's blood doesn't mean it's his.

She didn't fool herself. Her knees felt like the bones had been pulled out of them, and she sunk into the soft snow.

What if he wasn't dead? What if he were badly injured? What if he needed her?

She'd seen the other car, the other crime scene, where all that remained of the victims was a blood splatter, similar to this one. Though she knew precisely what she'd find inside, she still forced herself to stand and make her way over the bank and down to the car.

What if he'd been with someone else, and the blood belonged to them? What if Vince crouched, terrified, on the passenger floor, hurt and unable to rescue himself?

Even though she knew that wasn't the case, she opened the

door, gagging on the slaughterhouse smell. The passenger window was open, and snow buried the front seat. Where snow didn't cover, though, was blood. There wouldn't be a way to know if the blood belonged to him, because if it were like any of the others, the DNA was swept clean, and all that remained was sterile and impersonal. Blood coated the inside of the car, tacky, maroon and stinking. It glazed the plastic barricade between the backseat and the front.

The car was devoid of life. She hadn't needed it, but a grande Starbucks cup in the center console told her the car was his. She'd already known.

Didn't mean it was him. She thought of the myriad movies where no body meant the hero came striding back at the end to save the day. You can't assume someone is dead if you don't see a corpse. The greater number of real police cases she'd worked on provided a counterpoint: More often than not, in real life, the missing person was dead, whether you found their bleached skeleton or not.

The icy wind drained the warmth from her body, and she let Vince's door ease closed. It wasn't really his door. She knew someone from the state police would be along as soon as the weather cleared to bring the car back to the barracks. It would be cleaned and reissued to another trooper.

Lee gazed around the woods. The falling snow obscured any tracks, any evidence of a struggle or an attack. The wind relented for a few moments, and the only sound became a miniscule plopping as snow fell from evergreen branches. Then the wind took up again with a howl, and she headed back to the Jeep, trudging through knee-deep snow.

Inside, she cranked up the Jeep's heat.

Vince. Dead.

Maybe not—maybe the blood wasn't his. The fairy-tale part of her brain kept insisting on this hopeful outcome, but she knew it couldn't be.

A sob squeaked from between her lips.

"Y-you okay?" Mary Beth asked, through chattering teeth.

"The trooper in the car was my...friend. My really good friend." Tears escaped her eyes, and she wiped them away.

Mary Beth took her hand.

"You're a cop?"

"Forensics."

"Dennis Clarke? Was my boyfriend. Friend. Same deal."

Lee's heart rent at the news. "I'm so sorry."

"Do you know what happened?"

"No. And you know, there aren't bodies. They could be alive." Lee knew this wasn't likely. But she had to say it.

Mary Beth squeezed. Normally Lee didn't like touching, but she needed it now. "They're gone. You know that. It's a lot of blood. Too much."

Though she was afraid if she stopped, the Jeep's mighty tires would never find purchase; she pulled it to the side of the road, put it in neutral, and yanked up the emergency brake.

She sobbed, letting Mary Beth hold her. She talked more than she ever did to anyone. She told Mary Beth he was married, that she knew she was fooling herself; it couldn't really ever be anything. She knew she'd have to break it off, because he never would, but she didn't want him to be dead.

Mary Beth was a good listener.

"I'm so sorry," Lee said when she'd cried herself out. "I mean it. I never do this. I never spill my guts and—"

"It's okay. You distracted me from how cold I am."

"Let's head back to the diner and figure out what we're doing from there." In the minutes they'd been stopped, snow encroached on the Jeep from all sides, a thick layer on the hood and windshield. The wipers fought their way through. The tires protested moving at first, and spun a bit, but they finally caught and Lee carefully merged onto the road. She could hardly see anything, and crept along, hoping oncoming drivers would see her.

22 - MARY BETH

The feeling began to creep back into Mary Beth's fingers and toes, burning, unpleasant, hot. She rubbed her hands together in front of the Jeep's vent. Normally the ride from her place into town only took ten minutes, but the roads were worse than she'd ever seen them. The gray sky matched the snow, and the whole place had an unearthly, winter storm light. The plows either hadn't been out for a while, or couldn't compete with the falling snow.

She couldn't bring herself to tell what she'd seen. What the other woman had seen. Lee found her, sitting in the road, frozen. What Mary Beth would have been had Lee not come along? She couldn't imagine locking eyes with this stranger—this very personable, very nice stranger—and spewing such insanity. She'd try Jason. He might believe her.

"I can't wait to get inside and get warm. If everyone's holed up inside, and no one's out, we can wait for the snow to stop."

"No." Lee stared out the windshield, intent. "There are people out. The cops, the EMTs, the snowplow drivers. The same thing could happen to any of them. We go back to the diner and figure our next steps, but it's got to be soon."

She had a point, but Mary Beth would have been pretty happy to wait out the storm. No streetlights greeted them from the main street in town.

"I lose power a ton out at my place. But here? It almost never goes out." What passed for a downtown in Rocky Rhodes very rarely lost power. It didn't feel right—the storm shouldn't have knocked out the town's power.

Yellow lights peeked through the swirling snow at the diner, though. "Jason has a generator," Mary Beth explained.

"Jason's prepared for everything."

"He fought in the war. Or wars. He likes to plan ahead."

"Good."

As they neared the diner, Mary Beth saw something on the door. It caught in her throat and she almost couldn't speak. Breathing became hard, and she forced it out.

"The door. Look."

Blood. More blood. Fuck. Had the people in the diner... had whatever got Dennis and Lee's trooper gotten them? Nate's Explorer out front. She could only hope it got him, too.

Lee slowed the Jeep. "Oh my god," she whispered.

"It got them?"

"No. It's not enough blood. Something violent happened, but it's not the same as the others. I'm going to park around back."

"Yeah." Mary Beth directed her around the next intersection. The dirt parking lots behind the downtown sat on the bank of the Penquis creek, and every spring, almost without fail, it would overflow its banks and flood the lot. Today it lay dormant, iced over since mid-December, the same gray as the skies.

Mary Beth directed Lee to a cheery green painted door.

"Can we get in?"

"Depends."

Lee parked the Jeep and the women got out. The generator, protected by a chain-link fence, hummed loudly to their left. There wasn't a handle on the outside of the door, but it sat ajar. Delicious smells and warm air wafted out. Mary Beth's bad feeling intensified. Doors weren't just left open in the winter. It was damned cold out here, and you wanted to keep that inside.

Lee reached for the door.

"Do you have a gun?" Mary Beth said.

"No."

"You don't carry one?"

"I take samples. Most of the time, I'm in the lab. I don't even do field work usually. We were short staffed and...Vince thought it would be an easy one. A chance for us to get away." She stared at her boots, and her eyes started to fill up.

"No worries. We probably won't need it."

Mary Beth tried to think of all the perfectly reasonable expectations there could possibly be for the blood on the diner door. She couldn't come up with much.

Lee opened the door, and Mary Beth snuck in after her. The lights were on inside, but it seemed dark, cavelike. She hadn't realized how bright all that grayness outside was. They paused, aware that the daylight would give them away. The inside of the diner seemed silent. Warm, too, a striking temperature change from the storm outside. They stomped snow off their boots. Mary Beth tried to do it as quietly as she could. She didn't want to make noise.

Jason should be back here.

Lee pointed to the floor near one of the two swinging doors. Mary Beth hoped they weren't all dead. She didn't know what she would do if more familiar faces vanished from her life.

"You said they were okay when you left?" she asked.

Lee nodded, and spoke in a hushed tone. "Jason was here and starting to open the diner. He expected Angela in any minute, some folks started coming in."

Mary Beth peered through the window where Angela passed the orders. People—scared people—sat at the booths silent. Nate stood by the door, standing over a body. She couldn't tell whose it was, though it looked too big to be Ange's and too female to be Jason's.

Nick Larabee, sitting at one of the booths, caught her eye. She shook her head no, but Nate saw Nick's face light up. Mary Beth ducked, and let herself drop to the floor.

A bullet flew through the space her head occupied only moments before. The boom of the gunshot thundered through the little diner, and Mary Beth clapped her hands over her ears. She sucked in deep breaths. He'd tried to shoot her. Tried to kill her. Wanted her dead.

It was a strange feeling, knowing someone wanted her to die. It fluttered around in her head, a panicked thought on broken wings.

"Is it Nate?" Lee asked.

Mary Beth, unable to form words, nodded.

"So where are Jason and Angela?"

Mary Beth shook her head.

"I have a plan," Lee told her. Lee whispered her idea, to which Mary Beth said, flatly, "No way."

"You have a better idea?"

"I can't—"

"Sure you can."

Lee was pretty and athletic, with big blue eyes. She looked like a frigging Disney princess. Would her plan work, though?

"I'm going. You're okay."

"Wait—"

Lee slipped out the back. She would enter the diner from the front, and while she kept Nate's attention, Mary Beth would charge from the kitchen, and tackle him. She'd never tackled anyone in her life. Her hands shook, and she felt intensely, bizarrely, aware of her chipped nail polish. He wanted her *dead*.

She inched herself over to the stainless steel swinging door and waited. She relied solely on her ears, waiting for the tinkle of the opening door, and whatever Nate's reaction might be.

She waited. Waited. How long did it take to walk around the building? Lee took forever. Mary Beth's tense muscles screamed at her, she was ready to go and all the adrenaline pumping through her had no outlet. She spent her moments—and surely it couldn't have been more than five minutes—poised and ready.

The bell tinkled and she heard screaming.

Mary Beth launched herself from the kitchen.

Nick followed her lead, but somehow wasn't fast enough— he played for Greenville's football team, and he was good.

Lee stepped in, shivering, and started screaming when she saw the gun and the blood. And she screamed fucking loud.

She captured Nate's attention and Mary Beth hit him from behind, knocking him face-first onto the diner floor. The gun dropped from his hand and fired when it hit the floor, a round discharging and taking one ricochet before lodging in a mounted trout on the wall.

Lee cut off her scream like someone had unplugged her, but Callie, who most likely came in with Ginger, took up the mantle.

Nick landed on Nate a moment after Mary Beth did, and she was way too close to too many people. Did she smell bad? Nate certainly did. The thoughts were stupid, she knew it, but couldn't control where her brain went.

Even if Nate were down, there was still that...something in the woods.

Nate made a stupid whimpering sound and started to turn, but Nick pulled back his fist and drilled him. The punch made a terrible snapping sound, a one-two effect as Nick's fist hit Nate's head, then Nate's head hit the floor again.

His eyes slipped closed.

"Nice job, Mary Beth! I knew you could do it!" Lee said.

Only a handful of patrons were in the diner, but they all crowded around Lee and Mary Beth. Everyone talked at once, and Lee held up her hand to quiet them.

"Jason was shot," Ms. Perron said.

Mary Beth looked down at the body. Closer, she could tell who it was. She clapped a hand to her mouth. Ginger. Fuck, no. Ginger was her friend, no matter how shitty she could be sometimes.

Mark Haddon laid a coat over Ginger's upper body. The closest they could get to respect for the dead around here. Callie darted in, reaching for her.

"You can't do that!"

Mark held Callie back and tried to comfort her.

Mary Beth looked around. Where was Jason? She couldn't believe he'd been shot.

"Where is he?" Lee asked.

"Angela took him in the back."

"They're not back there," Mary Beth said.

Lee pushed through the swinging doors and called back "The storeroom! Angela, Jason, can you hear me? It's Lee. Nate's down."

It would be a whole lot nicer when they locked Nate in the room and Angela and Jason were out here.

Unless... She'd seen Ginger's face, a bullet through her eye. She didn't want to see Jason in the same way. She couldn't. Wouldn't. She wanted to go back to her trailer, to hell with what waited in the woods. No more people she cared about dead.

"Help me, please," Lee shouted into the diner.

Mary Beth went, dreading what she would find.

The storeroom door hung open. Relief flooded her so hard she thought her bladder might spring a leak. Her knees threatened to give out and she had to grab the counter for support. Jason stood between Mary Beth and Angela, leaning on them, but walking on his own.

Now that she knew Jason was okay, and Nate was unconscious, all she could think about was the...thing...outside. She wanted to tell them. She opened her mouth to tell them, but she let it close. She couldn't do it. They'd think she was insane.

"Grazed me," he was saying. Blood covered his face. "I have a thick fucking skull." They sat him down, and Angela went to work cleaning the blood off his face.

Nick and Mark dragged Nate to the storeroom and threw him inside. He made a meat-bag thud as he hit the ground. The door made a supremely satisfying sound as Mark threw the lock.

23 – LEE

The storeroom door closed with a metallic thud. Lee wished she were anywhere but here. She missed the quiet sterility of her lab, doing rock-paper-scissors with the girl in the next desk to see who would run for Starbucks. That act generally made up the high point of the conflict of her day. Not walking into a diner and finding corpses. It was different, somehow, when she was called to a scene. She knew what to expect. That was forensic Lee, not human being Lee. People close to her weren't part of that.

When she closed her eyes, she could only see the blood in Vince's car.

With a shudder, the generator quit, plunging the kitchen into darkness.

Jason cursed under his breath, and headed for the back door.

"Wait!" Mary Beth cried. "Don't go out there."

"I have to fire up the genny."

"But...listen."

Outside were heavy thuds, a metallic crunching. Sounds implying the generator was done for.

"Let's check on the people in the diner."

"But the generator."

"Please, Jason, don't go out there," Angela said. Lee wondered if she were using his so-obvious feelings for her to keep him safe.

In the dining room, a bloody streak on the linoleum floor marked where the redheaded girl had been dragged to her resting place.

"There's something out there. I saw it moving in the snow,"

said Mr. Cleere. "Couldn't tell what it was."

A boy, maybe nine, stood. "I have to go out there to see her."

"Jamie, sit down," his mother said. Tears brimmed in her eyes and her face was pale.

"Have to go see her. She's out there."

"What are you talking about—"

A man walked out of the diner, the bell tinkling behind him. All the other men stood at the window, staring out at the gray afternoon, transfixed, swaying.

"Jason?" Lee snapped her fingers in front of his face.

"Yeah? I'm okay. But she's out there. It's too cold, the storm's too strong. Someone's got to go save her." He sounded coherent, the words made sense.

"That guy's on it. He just left."

"But I *need* to save her."

Jason pulled his sleeve out of Lee's grip and moved toward the door. Jamie pulled away from his mother and scurried outside ahead of Mr. Cleere.

Angela put herself in front of Jason.

"Don't leave me," she said.

"I'll be back. You're safe and warm in here. What if it were you out there? I'd never leave you to freeze. And I won't let her. I'll be right back."

Jason left, followed by the last man in the diner. The remaining group of women blinked at one another.

Jamie's mother went out after him.

"Just sit tight," Lee said, and opened the door to the blizzard force winds. Snow robbed her of all sight. It fell from the sky and it blew in huge gusts.

"You need goggles and a snow machine," Angela said. "My dad's place is a block away, we've got them there."

There were stories in North Dakota of ranchers who'd tried to make it from the house to the barn to feed the animals, and wound up lost in distances of twenty, thirty feet. Sometimes their frozen corpses wouldn't be found until spring. Even if Jason's Jeep were up here, she didn't think it would make it through the snow. Angela was right, only a snowmobile would cut through the terrain.

Lee went to the table where Mary Beth sat. "I'm going with Angela. Going after them."

"You shouldn't. The weather's too bad. And..." Her voice trailed off.

"And what?"

"Nothing. Be careful. Do you have a gun?"

"No."

"Take Nate's?"

Lee looked around for it. It wasn't a bad idea. She'd been to the range with trooper friends lots of times, but by no means would she consider herself a good shot. She didn't see the gun anywhere. They hadn't let him take it in the storeroom, had they?

"Angela, do you know what happened to Nate's gun?"

"Jason took it."

"Dammit."

No gun for Lee. Honestly it was for the best. She would have shot herself in the foot anyway. She nodded to Mary Beth, who slouched miserably in one of the booths.

Angela cut out ahead of her, and Lee had no choice but to follow. They held hands so they didn't get separated. It reminded her of middle school, of being a girl, the buddy system. She hoped Mary Beth was all right back in the diner.

The wind chewed through her coat and her hat, and before too long she was shivering. Angela might have tried to speak, but the gusts stole her voice. It felt like they walked forever. There were moments when the storm stole the town from them, even though they walked down a street with buildings on both sides.

Angela wrenched from Lee's grasp and ran. Lee entertained a momentary thought of panic, of being left alone out here, and followed.

Angela's door hung open, snow already starting to pile in her living room. She cried out "Daddy" and bolted room to room, tracking piles of snow with her. Lee stood in the kitchen, trying to stomp the snow off her clothes and boots.

"It's taken all the men?" She phrased it as a question, but it wasn't one—all the men were gone.

Who...what...would take all the men?

"The garage," Angela said. She paused in the hall closet, and took out an adult-sized snowsuit. "It's my dad's—can you make it work? It's all we've got."

Lee nodded, shrugging into the too-big suit and zipping it to her chin. She donned heavy gloves, a better hat, and a pair of ski goggles. Inside the house, even though the door had been open, she started to sweat.

They went to the garage where it would be colder.

Two Arctic Cats sat in the gloom, vibrantly colored and ready to pounce. The snowmobile Angela sat on had belonged to her mother. It was purple and green, iridescent like a jewel. Angela's father's looked more like a hornet, yellow and black.

Lee took Angela's arm. Through the layers of glove and snowsuit it felt like holding a pillow. "You know we might be too late."

"It's my father and it's Jason. I have to try."

Angela opened the garage door and started both engines.

"Have you ridden before?"

"Once when I was a kid."

"Throttle, brake, kill switch, hand-warmer switch." Angela pointed to all the components. "No clutch, no stalling to worry about."

Lee straddled the yellow and black machine, loud color jaggedly splashed over the sleek visage. It thrummed between her legs. The storm swirled in through the open garage door. Outside was a wall of angry white, churning and eternal. Lee couldn't remember blue skies, green leaves, or yellow sun. Only the storm.

"Do you have a plan?" Lee shouted to be heard over the engines and the howling wind.

"Get Jason back. Get my dad back."

"Let's start at the Tebbs farm. He was the first to go missing."

Angela seemed to think for a moment, and nodded. They roared out into an afternoon dark as dusk.

24 - Mary Beth

Mary Beth sat in one of the booths, Callie sitting on the other side, her face ghostly.

"But where did they go?" she asked for maybe the hundredth time. Mary Beth toyed with a few different options, punching her, locking her in the room with Nate. Throwing her outside.

She pushed her thoughts instead to the thing she'd seen. By now, she'd convinced herself she hadn't actually seen it. Inside her mind an ongoing argument festered between what she labeled "sane Mary Beth" and "batshit crazy Mary Beth."

She should have told Lee about it, even if it was crazy.

Batshit crazy Mary Beth made the compelling argument: Something out there in the storm was reducing people—apparently only men—to a fine, bloody mist. If not the giant, grublike thing, then what?

No answer presented itself. *There's a killer in the woods who carries a jet engine, and likes to feed his victims through it, obviously.* Nope, not buying that one, either. She was hungry, but no one else seemed to be moving toward food, so she let herself feel it. She didn't want to be the fat survivor who ate all the time. If she got out of this, and the chances were good, since the thing only killed dudes, she would move away. She would lose 85 pounds. She would run and go outside. She would do volunteer work and have real friends she didn't have to buy with drugs.

It all seemed pretty scary.

A rhythmic thumping came from the back room. Nate was awake, and he wanted out. Mary Beth agreed with Jason. Should have killed him while they had the chance. Now she sat trapped here with Mrs. Brautagan, a soccer mom who'd curled into a ball at a booth; Callie, who'd never been much better than useless; and two old Q-tips who looked like they clearly remembered the Kennedy administration.

If Nate came out, it was on her to deal with him. Jason should have killed him. Somehow, Angela had never appreciated the extent to which he was slime. And now he was killing people? Sorry, dude, you've waived your right to consume resources.

"Where did they go?" Callie asked.

"Just shut up."

"What? Maybe we should go there too. See if they need help."

"No." As much as it hurt to admit, she knew she'd slow them down. If they were running, she'd start wheezing. It was probably more the cigarettes than the weight. And the lack of practice. She stood, feeling her knees pop, and went to the kitchen.

Thump.

Thump.

Thump.

She checked the door and found it locked. Then the thumping stopped. She heard a quiet, metallic scraping sound. It took her breath, drenched her in fear. The kitchen was dark since the power went out, only the light from a red exit sign on one wall, and a harsh glare of a security light illuminated the room. The emergency light illuminated a pile of boxes, and not much of the light spilled where a person might actually need to see. It pretty much only made things worse.

Another scraping sound, almost gentle. She thought about saying "Hello," but didn't want to hear her own voice. With the power and the heat out, the temperature dropped. She could see her breath back here.

Something small fell from the ceiling and tinkled to the floor next to her. She dropped to a knee to pick it up...a screw? As she looked up to see where it came from, a heavy shape descended on her, sending her to the slick tile floor.

Nate. His face was bloody and bruised, one eye puffed almost closed. His hair stood in wild tufts, and every vestige of handsomeness had fled from his face. A crazy glint sparkled in his eyes. Strong hands found their way around her throat. He banged her head on the floor and she saw bright white stars. She flailed at him, slapping at him with her hands, then she groped for something, anything to hit him with. Something with some substance. She longed for a good, full breath.

Her fingers closed around something, the leg of a stool, and she dragged it over, felled it on him with a clatter. It distracted him, at least, and he relaxed his grip on her throat. She sucked in a ragged lungful. The air burned, but had never tasted so sweet.

She pushed herself up against him, knocking him off balance. She outweighed him, and for once in her pathetic life, it was an advantage. Now that she had some leverage, she swung back and punched him, her fist making a good, solid contact with his face.

He groaned. At least he wasn't talking. She didn't think he could handle the vitriol he spewed.

He came at her again, and she half dodged him, so he collided with her hip. They tumbled to the floor together, and she landed on top of him, pinning him down. She used her elbows as best she could to stab into him. She reached for his eyes with her fingernails, but he kept blocking her.

The kitchen doors swung open, and Callie stood in the doorway, her eyes wide, her stupid face slack.

"Help me," moaned Mary Beth.

Nate grunted.

"Help me!"

Callie just stared.

Nate wriggled out from under Mary Beth and scrambled to his feet. He overturned a metal prep table that clattered loudly to the floor. He lunged at Callie.

"Run!" Mary Beth shrieked.

Callie was too stupid, though, and she very slowly lifted her arms in front of her to ward him off.

Nate threaded his fingers through her thick hair and held her like a shield in front of him.

"Where did they go?" He growled, the words rumbling in his throat.

Mary Beth shook her head. "All the men took off. And

Angela and Lee went after them."

"I *know* all the men left. Where did they *go*?" The growl reduced to a whine. "I couldn't follow and now I don't know which way to go."

"I don't know."

Nate brought his free hand down on a stainless steel counter, inches away from the still-hot grill. It made a loud clanging noise.

"I have to—don't know where they went." He twisted Callie's face around, wrenching her neck. "Where did they go?"

Callie could barely speak. Tears oozed down her cheeks, and her mouth was thick with spit. "Don't know. I'm sorry. Nate, I—"

"You're useless. Both useless!"

He shook her and she whimpered.

"*Where?*" he shouted, whirling her around, laying her cheek on the grill. Callie's scream filled the room, high and pure, almost musical in its clarity and tone. The smell of cooking meat and melting plastic filled the room. Mary Beth's stomach heaved. She brought a hand to her mouth.

Nate shoved Callie down to the floor and glared at Mary Beth. Callie landed in a puddle, the burned side of her face pressed into the cool tile. Mary Beth took a tentative step toward her, but Nate moved in. "Take me to them. Find them and take me there."

"She needs a doctor."

Nate kicked her. "Fuck her. Fuck a doctor. Doctor's probably already with the rest of the men. I'm stuck here with these fucking bitches. Fucking women."

Giving up Callie as a lost cause, Mary Beth inched away. Nate reached for something. A slight scrape of metal on metal. A knife, glinting in the bright emergency light.

"Find them and take me to them."

25 – LEE

Against her wishes, against her better judgment, Lee had to admit the snowmobile was kind of fun. When she'd been driving the Jeep, the vehicle seemed to be fighting the weather. The Arctic Cat didn't try to make the snow into something it wasn't—it skimmed along the surface, the treads humming underneath her. Through the goggles, and tucked away in the warm snowsuit, she felt she could appreciate the beauty of the storm and the forest. She didn't want to. She shoved all the positive emotions aside. Reminded herself of the death and the cold.

Promised herself a week in Key West.

They mostly stuck to the roads. Any tracks Jason and the others might have made were barely visible in the blowing, falling snow. It all started at the Tebbs farm, on the outskirts of town, almost over in one of the unnamed incorporated townships. There had to be something there she and the police had missed the day before, a clue, anything.

She rode, following Angela, scanning the gloomy afternoon for any sign of the men. Would they freeze out here? They certainly would if she and Angela didn't do anything to help them. She squeezed the hand warmers, grateful for their heat. Angela hunched forward on her seat. She didn't look natural, didn't seem to be enjoying her ride. Lee focused on her taillights.

Lee couldn't tell how long they'd been riding, but her butt had started to ache and her thighs protested from being held apart. She suspected she was a wimp, her thighs were unaccustomed to the ride, and they hadn't actually been out all that long.

Angela slowed. A massive snow bank, left from the plow's

last valiant attempt at clearing the road, blocked the Tebbs's mile-long driveway. Something black poked out from the snow, almost entirely buried in fluffy white. Lee stepped off the snowmobile, leaving it rumbling behind her. God, standing felt good. She made her way through calf-deep snow, and pulled out a man's glove.

"We can go over," Angela shouted. "Just be careful." She inched up the steep hill, moving so slowly Lee feared she'd fall back. Angela disappeared over the big bank. Lee felt a kinship with her machine, gunned the engine, and pushed it up and over the snow bank. The ground dropped away from her, and an actual laugh slipped out of her mouth in the moment before the snowmobile landed in deep, fluffy snow. Vince would want her to laugh. The thought sobered her.

Angela headed up the driveway. The snow deeper snow made traction harder to come by. It didn't look like the driveway had been plowed since the storm began.

They had to slow their pace, but they pushed ahead into the blustery wind and blowing snow. Going faster on the main road protected them from some of the crosswinds, but now those same gusts threatened to throw Lee off her ride. She hunkered down and pushed forward. Two cars sat parked outside the little cabin, but no smoke curled from the chimney. Even so, the door opened, and a tired old face peered out.

Mr. Tebbs? Lee thought wildly. If he was all right, then Vince might be, too.

"You're too late."

The voice that cut through the storm was a woman's, and Lee's heart sank.

"Too late for what?" Angela asked.

"To save the men."

"Where did they go?"

Lee stayed silent.

The woman pointed out toward the woods, a trail between looming evergreens. The wind seemed quieter now, and if Lee wasn't mistaken, the snow had let up slightly. So there were some miracles.

"That's where it all started."

"What are you talking about?" Lee asked.

"Last week. The meteor."

"What meteor? I never heard anything about that."

"Why would you?" the old woman asked. "Who watches the sky in Rocky Rhodes?"

Next to Alaska or Montana, Maine was a dot on a map, a tiny state. But people didn't appreciate how big the woods were up in Piscataquis and Aroostook counties. You could walk for days and not see signs of human life. The forest primeval closed in on all sides. And the woman was right—these woods, and the quaint towns nestled in them, were all but forgotten. Hunters visited them, other outdoors enthusiasts, but mostly they remained pristine and unchallenged.

"Tell us what happened?" Lee asked.

"All I know is there was a meteor, and then Clarence disappeared. I found the first blood a bit later. Great lakes of it. I started back to the cabin when I saw the creature."

"I'm sorry, what?" Creature? Meteor? What the hell was going on here?

"Something fell from the sky. Something huge, and it only likes to feed on men. You're too late to save the ones it's called."

"It took everyone from the town."

Sadie shook her head. "It's back down the path. Seems to be holed up around the old ranger's station. Don't know what it'll do to you women. Doesn't seem to care much for our taste."

"Let's go," Angela said.

"We don't know what we're getting in to. How do we know what will—"

"Jason and my dad are out there. I'm not going to let them die."

"Be careful. We at least want to get a look at it first. To see what we're up against."

But Angela had already restarted her Arctic Cat, and pushed it out back toward the trail. In the protection of the tall, ancient pines, they started to see boot prints.

Around the next bend they found an older man, collapsed in the snow.

Angela braked hard and her snowmobile skidded, but

she regained control and stopped. By the time Lee got to her, Angela knelt in the snow next to the man. "This is Mr. Pullman. He teaches geography at the school. Get him back to Sadie, back where it's warm. He doesn't have much time."

Lee knew she was right, he had to go back. But Lee had more training, was in a better position to go ahead. She agreed, and helped Mr. Pullman onto her sled, though. She knew if it were her men, her family out there, she would be damned if she would let some stranger be the one to save them.

The cold man snuggled into her, barely able to speak. She gunned the engine and pushed as hard as she dared back to Sadie's cabin.

Sadie held her door for them, looking disapprovingly down at the slightly frostbitten man. He thanked them profusely, and Sadie gave them a cup of coffee to warm up. Lee couldn't wait to get back out there, to help Angela. But she'd said taught science.

"My ankle," he said. "I couldn't go any farther. And they left me there. I was only down for a bit when I realized we were all crazy. What happened to me? To all of us?"

"I'm not sure," Lee said.

"I was so sure there was a woman, lost. She needed me to save her..."

"But all of the men went. All of them from the town."

The snow around them was trampled, trodden down by many feet. Boot prints, sneaker prints, even one bare footprint littered the snow. Lee wondered about the man with no shoes, and hoped the best for him.

"Did you see a creature?" She remembered the older woman's words, perhaps Mr. Pullman had seen something.

"Creature? No, there was a woman. A woman in white. It was the damndest thing...I thought I had to save her."

"You're safe now," Lee said. "I have to go after Angela. I have to help her."

Leaving Sadie's cabin, the cold slapped her in the face as she stepped out. She was tired. Didn't want to get back on the machine and ride, go back into the woods and face danger. If Vince had been out there, she would have wanted the help. She started the engine, and headed down the path.

26 – ANGELA

All around her, the snow began to lighten. The wind receded, and on the forest trail the snowflakes began to look almost picturesque. A churning, gnawing knot thrashed in Angela's chest. Every so often, protected by the trees, she would see a boot print, some sign of passing traffic.

Something moved in the forest up ahead. It had been a long time, years, since she'd been out here. She remembered coming this way on a fishing trip with her dad, the canoe in the back of his pickup truck. He was out here somewhere in the cold. And Jason was with him.

"Hello?" she shouted into the winter afternoon, but the sound of her engine heralded her presence more than her voice could. The forest seemed more silent, more still. There weren't any birds out in the storm to be silenced, but something about this place tickled a lizard part of her brain, somewhere deep down at the stem. Something lurked out here, watching and waiting.

She killed the Arctic Cat's engine and listened. Off to her left, a pile of snow fell from a tree and she jumped.

"Dad?" she shouted. The snow muffled and absorbed her sound, and the forest returned to silence. She wanted to go home. Wanted none of this to have happened.

Was this her punishment? Had she brought this on all of them? She touched her stomach through the snowsuit and told herself she was being crazy. She licked her chapped lips, and started the engine. She knew the trail would fork up ahead and the right path would lead to the lake. The left path headed to an old ranger station they'd stopped using in the '80s. Kids, herself included on more than one occasion, used it to screw or smoke up. The tower still stood, but the wood was spongy and soft and rotted through in places. Billy Cramer put a foot through a rung on the ladder a few years back and almost fell twenty-five feet to the stone platform below.

The memories were easier than facing the uncertainty. She debated which way to go. She hoped, for her dad's and Jason's sake, they were in the ranger station. It would provide at least some shelter from the elements.

She hated how loud the snowmobile was, and at the fork she turned it toward Rocky Rhodes and killed the engine. She left the key in the ignition. If someone stole it...well, likely she'd have bigger problems. She moved forward on foot, getting off the trail and slipping through the snow-laden evergreen boughs. The element of surprise was her only advantage, and she didn't want to lose it.

About a hundred yards from the ranger station, she saw the first red patch of snow. She stifled a cry into her heavy-duty glove. How many of the men were out here? The more were here, the better chance her dad and Jason were all right.

As she crept farther, she saw another blotch, and another. She rounded the final bend in the trail and froze in her tracks. One wall of the ranger's station lay collapsed and crumbled, and something big huddled inside. She saw twenty or so men standing around, some inside, some out, all focused raptly on the thing blocking her view. They barely moved, stamping their feet against the cold, blowing into cupped hands. She scanned their backs for her father and Jason. Jason was easy, his ponytail hung out of a knit cap down the back of his red jacket. Her father was harder to identify. A few of the guys wore the furred bomber caps like he'd always worn. She had him narrowed down to one of two tall men, both wearing a teal L.L. Bean jacket.

The thing in the station, though. It...defied logic. She found she couldn't look at it for too long or it confounded her. It looked like a huge grub. And a strange, malformed thing hovered in front of it. The men stared at the thing transfixed, like they'd seen the second coming of Christ.

She had to find a way to get their attention, to pull them away.

The grub made a bassy, resonant sound like a foghorn, and all the men started talking, each of them addressing the strange thing.

Angela made her way around to get a closer look. She kept to the cover of the pine boughs. Jason stood off to the side, maybe she could catch his eye, motion him away from the crowd. She moved as quietly as she could in the fluffy snow, never taking her eyes off the grub. Its face—if you could call it a face—was pinched and black, with pointed teeth hanging free.

As she watched, an unidentifiable man moved forward, away from the rest. The crowd let out a jealous mutter, collectively wishing they were the ones called to the strange blob.

The blob hovered, moving almost rhythmically, like a strand of kelp in the sea. Underneath it...*her?*... blood stained the snow.

The summoned man wrapped his arms around blob, cradling it to his chest. Bringing his mouth to it. Kissing it. While it distracted him, the grub's tail snaked around. A sick, man-size spine lanced out from the creature's tail. It came from above, piercing the man in the back, skewering him like a kebab. He didn't stop kissing the thing, running his hands over it, cupping its shapeless form and pressing himself against it. He never stopped, not even as he started to swell in his winter clothes. Blood soaked them from the inside, adding to the charnel mess in the snow at his feet. He puffed up to about twice his size and the grub poked its toothy black face in through his side. It seemed to drink for a moment, and the man started to reduce like a water balloon with a leak. Then he popped, spattering red fluid over the first row of men, the snow, and the white grub. One of the men in teal received the unholy bath. The grub's fat flanks rippled, and it seemed to grow bigger.

Angela bit her glove, trying not to scream.

27 - MARY BETH

Nate's knife dug into Mary Beth's hip, through layers of parka and sweater. Sweat trickled down her back, only serving to make her colder. They sat in Jason's Jeep. Nate leaned over her lap, head under the steering wheel, trying to hot-wire the vehicle into life. Jason had taken his keys with him when he headed for wherever he went.

Mary Beth imagined doing all sorts of things to Nate while he focused on the wires. Smashing his head into the steering wheel, throwing the door open and attempting escape...but in every case, she thought about the knife. If she didn't get it right the first time, he'd be on her. She kept seeing Callie's burned visage every time she closed her eyes. The girl blacked out, and now lay unconscious in the kitchen. Probably better that way.

The Jeep tried to start, but her foot wasn't on the clutch so it died. On her second try, Mary Beth coaxed it to life.

Nate sat up and prodded her with the knife. "Drive."

Her hands were shaking so hard she had to grip the wheel. "Where?" she croaked.

"Follow them!"

"Follow them where?"

"People leave trails, stupid. Follow them."

Her side hurt and she couldn't tell if it were blood or sweat she could feel pooling around her wound. She imagined the people lying dead in the diner, and commanded she stop making such a big deal over a little scratch.

She wished Dennis were here, and that wish hurt her more than anything Nate could do with the knife.

She stalled the Jeep and he poked her again. "Don't fuck this up, cow."

"Why can't you drive it yourself?" She immediately regretted saying it.

Nate fixed her with a cool stare. "Then what the fuck would I do with you? You drive, or you die."

The Jeep protested until she put it in four-wheel drive, then it easily came out of the parking space. She went around to the main road, slow going in the deep snow. She could barely see tracks, but she had an idea she knew where all the men had gone.

She pointed the car toward the old ranger station.

"Where are you taking us?"

"I'm following them."

"Following what?"

She took a chance. "Don't you see their tracks in the snow? They're faint, but they're there." It shut him up, so scared of being wrong. He was pathetic. Soon they clearly saw two snowmobile tracks in the snow, relatively fresh. It calmed Nate down.

"This is bullshit. All the men. And *Angela's* going, but I wasn't invited. You know what it was like being in that room? I couldn't get out. Bitch put me there."

"How did you know the men were going?" Mary Beth tried to keep him talking. He wasn't as scary and it was way easier to hate him when he ran his stupid, bullshit mouth.

"Are you kidding?"

"I'm not lucky enough to be a man, so I don't know what it was like."

He scoffed. "You know what fresh chocolate chip cookies smell like?"

"Yeah."

"And you know what sex smells like? Dennis did fuck you, didn't he?"

"Yes, I know what sex smells like." She wanted to rip Dennis's name out of Nate's vocabulary. Wanted him never to say it again.

"Don't talk about—"

He poked her with the knife again. Harder. It sliced through her skin and came away red tipped.

"I'll cut you to death if you speak again."

They rode along in silence, Mary Beth wondering if that would be so bad. Nate went on. "Anyway, it was like something in the middle. A perfect scent. And all those other fuckers got to go, but I didn't because Angela wanted it all for herself. Wanted them all for herself. But she's too good to carry my son. She killed him, you know."

Mary Beth was still trying to wrap her imagination around a combined chocolate chip cookie/sex smell, and how that could be anything but awful. It had intoxicated the men, compelled them. Even levelheaded, reasonable guys like Jason and Mr. Cleere. Had someone drugged them? She remembered the thing she'd seen in the woods. Had that thing drugged them? Now she drove right toward it.

Nate would make a good blood spatter.

Once a blizzard, now only fluffy flakes fell from the sky. Visibility increased, and the sky grew lighter. The Jeep bounced and shuddered its way down the snowy path. She knew she had to maintain a certain speed or they'd get stuck, but when she started going too fast, her control slipped. It was a balancing act. All a balancing act. It crossed her mind a few times to crash the Jeep on purpose, to roll it, or something, but Nate wore his seat belt, and she worried it wouldn't kill him. She'd be trapped by the steering column, and he'd get to cut her to death anyway.

She pushed on, past a small house. She got the impression there were people inside, holed up and afraid. The snowmobile tracks were thicker on the far side, like one of the machines had come and gone. The path ahead didn't look wide enough for the Jeep, and she stopped on a flat patch of ground, looking uncertainly at Nate.

"I think we go on foot."

"On foot? In this? No way. You drive."

"I don't think I can."

"I know you're a shit woman driver and all that, but do it."

She eased the Jeep forward. Branches scraped the sides like bony fingers. Sorry, Jason. The snow hid ruts in the road and rocks, and she bounced along, trying to follow the snowmobile trails. They had the right idea. She hoped she was right, and she was actually following the men. What would Nate do to her if she were only following some yokels out for a ride in the fresh snow?

They could hear the whine of the snowmobile engine up ahead.

28 - Lee

Lee pushed the snowmobile harder than she knew she should. She mostly stuck in Angela's trail, but when the skis left the packed snow, she felt her traction falter. She rounded a corner, and found the green and purple machine, sitting facing her. So where was Angela? Lee braked hard and skidded, lost control and stalled. She sat in the silent forest, listening to snow falling from the trees, the whisper of a gentle breeze through pine needles.

Angela had been right to get the snowmobile turned around for a hasty exit. Who knew what lay in front of them? Reluctant to make so much noise, Lee fired up her machine and got it turned around, parked next to Angela's. Only the thinnest layer of snow had accumulated on Angela's seat.

Her tracks were easy to follow, and Lee moved as quietly as she could in the gloom. She didn't know what time it was. Night came so early in the winter. The Weather Channel said each day grew slightly longer than the last, but she didn't notice.

She passed the first blood spot. The snow around it lay flattened, smoothed down by the passing of something large, something dragged? She wasn't sure. She tried to ignore the blood spots. She'd noticed from the first that they didn't smell quite right. Once you've smelled blood, it's easy to recognize the scent again. The blood in Rocky Rhodes was different, like a familiar song played slightly off key. She brought a glove to her nose, eager to smell anything else.

Up ahead she saw a tall tower, so rickety that it couldn't possibly be used anymore, wood and metal reaching to the sky. Below it she saw a dilapidated building, and the bright spots of all the men's winter coats. Lee stuck with Angela's tracks, staying low and out of cover. What lay in the building was another story. She tried to make sense of what she saw there, lying in the shadows like a huge, malignant slug. When Mrs. Tebbs said *creature*, Lee wasn't sure what she expected. This wasn't it. *Creature*, in her mind, implied fur. Mammalian. Something a biologist could identify. This thing couldn't be from her planet. Couldn't exist. She closed her eyes, expecting it to disappear when she opened them again.

It didn't.

She couldn't see what the men up ahead were doing, gathered around it. For a large group of people, they made little noise, giving the scene an eerie, funereal aspect. It made sense, she guessed. For a number of these guys, it *was* their funeral. She stared at the thing, aware it would have a starring role in her nightmares for the rest of her days. Amid the susurrations of the wind in the trees, she heard something else, something lower, rumbling. So out of place out here in nature that it took her a moment to realize what it was. A car.

Lee turned behind her, but she couldn't see it yet, something far down the path they'd come up. Anything much larger than a snowmobile would have a hard time on the trail they'd traveled. Lee hung back. A newcomer would change the dynamic of the scene. She searched the fringe of the trees for Angela.

She caught a blur of pink, and saw the girl darting out from cover.

No! She bit back the shout. She didn't want the men, or the creature, to notice her.

Angela darted out and caught Jason's sleeve. She pulled at him and he pulled back, irritated, almost, that she disturbed him. None of the other men glanced her way. Angela tugged a glove off, reached back, and slapped him across the face. It made a crisp crack in the wintery afternoon.

None of the men reacted, though Jason shook his head, looked around, brought a hand to his mouth. He followed Angela into the bushes. Lee rushed over to them, whipping branches out of her face. They tore at her like icy claws. Jesus, she hated the woods. She stepped in a pile of snow deeper than it looked, and twisted her knee. White spots of pain exploded in her vision.

Really? This was how she got hurt? Walking in fluffy snow? She'd seen people shot today, seen car accidents, and exploded blood. And she hurt herself walking in the snow.

When she reached them, Jason looked reduced. His eyes were haunted. He wrapped his arms around Angela and held her close. It wasn't a romantic clinging, more a clinging to life. He looked relieved to see Lee as well.

"I wanted her so bad. I still do. I almost can't help myself."

"Wanted what?" Lee asked. She glanced at the quivering, glistening grub monster. She rubbed at her aching knee, and hoped she wouldn't have to run anywhere.

"Her." Jason pointed at the shapeless mass out in front. Another man wrapped his arms around it, holding it. Another willing sacrifice.

"The...thing?" Angela asked.

Jason shivered. "No. The woman out in front. Now that I'm away, I can't see her as well. Hang on." He took a few steps away, knelt on the ground, and whitewashed himself, working the fluffy snow into his face. He stood, shook off, reminiscent of a dog, and returned to them, cheeks bright red.

Jason panted and Lee wanted to tell him to calm down. He was close to hyperventilating. "That's fucked up." He struggled for a few breaths. "The monster vanishes, the other guys vanish, it's just you and her. I never got my chance with her..."

"Thank God," Angela said.

Jason looked like a high school kid with a crush, peering at her.

"So we need to go slap those other guys, and they'll be all right?" Angela asked.

A Jeep—Jason's Jeep—flying into the clearing interrupted her thought.

Jason glanced at Lee. "Who's driving my truck?"

Lee recognized Mary Beth's white face behind the wheel, and a smaller man beside her.

"It's Nate," Angela whispered.

The men turned at the loud sound of the Jeep's approach,

and the grub-monster roared in fury. She didn't like being interrupted. They could hear Nate screaming at Mary Beth, and watched as she plowed the vehicle into the crowd. Only a few of the men had the wherewithal to get out of the way, she ran some of them down with sick crunches. The Jeep screeched to a stop before the grub, before the shapeless thing.

"Is she beautiful?" Angela asked.

"She's amazing," said Jason. "She keeps fading in and out for me...the blobby thing you guys see and the woman I see."

Nate stumbled from the passenger seat, and fell to his knees before the lure.

29 – ANGELA

Angela left Jason's side and moved closer so she could get a better look at her ex-boyfriend. She wondered how she could have loved him, how she could have found him attractive. He dropped to his knees in front of the thing and begged it to take him. Even Angela could see it turn its back on him. The grub had taken an interest in him herself. She lowered her massive head to him and roared, an earsplitting, ancient sound. He barely glanced at it, reaching out for the woman-thing.

"No!" Nate shouted, his voice ringing out in the winter air. He grabbed at it, and yanked it back. Angela flinched—he'd grabbed the blob-woman's shoulder in the same way as when she'd tried to walk away from him.

The remaining men grumbled discontent.

"He can't do that to her," Jason muttered. Lee held him back.

Nate took hold of the woman and shook her. Mr. Garvey, the kindly old man who'd run the little market for as long as Angela could remember, intervened, trying to pull Nate off the thing. Nate reached back and punched him. He returned his attention to the woman-thing, spinning her around. He'd done that to Angela, too. Now he grabbed what Angela presumed was her face, holding her by the chin.

"You don't walk away from me."

Nick Larabee, who was still in high school, pulled Nate off. He reached out to the woman by way of apology, then floored Nate with a punch. Kicked him. Angela's father joined him, then Casey Barthes, the mechanic. Mark Haddon, who liked to have a late breakfast at the diner. And Jesse St. Croix, an accountant who telecommuted to Portland, Boston, and New York. She couldn't see who was who anymore; they all descended or. her ex-boyfriend.

She told herself no matter how much of a shit he was, she couldn't let them do this, they'd kill him. But she stayed silent until Lee limped to her side, holding Jason's hand.

"We have to burn the station down. Heat should kill it."

"You'll hurt her," Jason said. "He hurt her!" Jason moved toward the mob, but Lee yanked him back.

Lee heard the crunch of tires on snow, but didn't look up until Angela spoke.

"What's she doing with the Jeep?"

30 - Mary Beth

It took a few minutes for Mary Beth's head to clear. She'd just killed maybe three people. Her hands shook, her breath stayed locked in her chest, only sneaking out in ragged gasps. She was a murderer.

She wasn't the only murderer here. Before her loomed the thing responsible for Dennis's death.

She watched the men descend on Nate Irving. She didn't want to say it helped her calm down, but it did. And once she felt calm, she started the Jeep. She turned her attention to the grub-monster. She locked eyes with it. *Dennis.*

"This isn't your place, bitch," she muttered. She revved the engine, got it ramped up to an angry whine. It leapt forward like a racecar when she pulled her foot off the clutch. She avoided the mob kicking the shit out of—killing—Nate. She stomped on the accelerator as hard as she could, and then the Jeep exploded into the old ranger's station taking down part of the collapsed wall. The grub-beast loomed larger and larger, filling the windshield, then she hit it. Jason had a big grille on the front of the Jeep, which impacted the thing's soft side first, squishing into it.

Mary Beth didn't stop accelerating. She pushed as hard as she could, felt a piece of the thing give way, buckle underneath her onslaught.

This fucking thing killed Dennis. The thought ricocheted around her head like a frantic bat. Dennis would be here if this thing had never come. She slammed the Jeep into reverse, and rammed it again.

31 – LEE

"Oh Jesus fuck," Jason said, as Mary Beth rammed the grub with the Jeep. For a split second, Lee thought he was upset about his truck, but seeing the other men's reactions, she realized the spell was broken. The men pulled away from the bloody mess that was Nate, seeming to come to their senses. Maybe he was still alive, but she doubted it.

Jason leaned on her, almost pulling her down. His weight jarred her knee, and the joint screamed. His eyes weren't right, he was teetering on the edge of losing his shit.

"Later," Lee said. "We have to burn this bitch down."

He nodded, seemed to come back to her, and helped her limp to the structure. He passed her a lighter from his pocket and she hoped the station's wood was old and dry enough to catch fire easily.

32 – ANGELA

"We have to help these people!" someone cried. Some of the men sobbed, some were taking action. Casey had a large branch and stabbed at the grub-thing. Her spiny tail waved wildly, narrowly missed Angela's father, but caught Mr. Garvey. He screamed, clawed at where it pierced his chest. His blue-mittened hands looked ineffective and childish swatting at it.

Her father saw her and ran to her, wrapping her in his arms, enveloping her.

Because it was what she said, because she couldn't think of anything else to say, she muttered, "I'm sorry!"

The ranger's station burned, little flickers of cheerful yellow and orange flames licking at the old walls. It started small, but grew greedy, the fire growing and devouring.

When the first flames touched the grub-monster, it threw its narrow head back and screamed. Everyone clapped their hands to their ears. The sound made Angela's fillings hurt.

The thing pulled its spine from Mr. Garvey. He flopped to the ground in a motionless pile.

33 - LEE

Lee limped to the fallen man, her limited medical skills not as useful as she hoped they might be here. Someone had to call for help. A rescue chopper—though not with this weather.

The fallen man seized on the ground, thick, bloody phlegm oozing from his lips. Something from the grub-beast's stinger poisoned him, ruined him from the inside. Blood and ichor began to leak from his eyes, his nose, even dribble from his ears onto the trampled snow.

Lee left him behind and went to Nate. He appeared a lost cause, battered and broken on the ground. His face was swollen, his right eye puffed shut, the left one staring off at an improbable angle. His mouth, partway open, showed broken, bloody teeth. She reached down and felt for a pulse, but found none.

She wished for a sheet, or something to pull over his face. Instead she turned and left him where he lay. She couldn't do anything for him.

The ranger station, once it had gotten the idea, began to burn. The grub-beast tried to squirm out, but Mary Beth cut it off with the Jeep, forcing it back, slamming into its albino visage. It reared up, its huge bulk filling the ranger's station. It let out a low, tonal sound—a battle cry. It waved its spine at the Jeep, stabbing downward. It struck the metal hood of the vehicle, and the spine broke with an audible snap. It uttered its cacophonous cry again. Mary Beth pushed the Jeep into it again. One of the major supports, licked red with flames, gave way with a groan and landed across the thing's back.

Jason put a hand on her shoulder.

"What do you see?"

"I think I see what you do. It's not doing its smell thing anymore, not that I can tell. I see a gross lump, and an even grosser monster."

She shivered. "It killed Vince. I mean, Sgt. Staghorn." She'd expected a kind of peace to come with the information. It didn't. He was still gone. Left behind a pretty wife and two little kids. She wondered if Mary Beth found closure.

"I think I'm going to try and get my Jeep," Jason said. "Get out of here, bring back help."

Lee nodded to him. Once the building collapsed on the thing, Mary Beth backed off, and sat idling, watching the fire, poised and ready to strike.

34 - MARY BETH

She jumped when someone tapped on the window, and even when she saw it was Jason; she still hunkered in the driver's seat, shaking. He came around and got in the passenger side. Nate had sat there. Nate was dead. Dead like the monster that killed Dennis. She took in the bodies scattered around the ranger station yard. Killed a lot of people.

"What was it?" she asked.

"Fucked if I know. You killed it real good, though."

She nodded.

"Mind if I drive?"

"Uh, no. That's cool. Sorry about your Jeep." She couldn't see the damage to the front end, but could imagine she'd done a number on it. She could see a massive dent in the hood where the spine hit. She'd see it arcing toward her in her dreams for the rest of her life. She shivered, almost convulsive, but not from the cold. She couldn't even feel the cold.

"Are you okay?"

"I hate this place."

"I know."

He squeezed her hand. "Let's switch spots, and I'll head into town. Try and raise the authorities."

"And tell them what?"

"Fucked if I know," he said again. "Tell them to send a coroner and an ambulance, let them sort it out."

Mary Beth found she didn't want to get out of the car, didn't want to be out there in the world with that thing. Somehow being in here felt safe and protected. They traded spots, Jason put a couple of the more badly wounded men in the backseat. He turned, and eased the Jeep toward town, as fast as the weather permitted. The seat belt rubbed where Nate jabbed her with the knife as she rotated in her seat and looked back and the burning ranger's station.

35 – Lee

The state police came. Then the FBI came. Then someone else came. She'd heard stories of *men in black*, and these men and women wore khakis and navy blue windbreakers, but they seemed awfully calm about the tractor-trailer-sized grub corpse in the charred-out ranger's station.

Lee's knee screamed, and she found herself exhausted in the absence of the adrenaline that had been with her most of the day.

They asked an infuriating series of questions, and didn't offer a lot of answers. One of them, a pixie-like blonde in a blue suit, gave her a final interview.

"I need to take your RV. I have to confiscate all of the results from any tests you've performed. I'll have it back to the Portland station in a few weeks."

Yeah right, Lee thought. She'd never see the RV again. "I don't suppose I can argue?"

She didn't smile, but looked the closest she'd come so far. "No. One of the troopers will give you a ride back to Portland."

"Okay."

The woman handed Lee a five-figure check. "This should take care of your immediate needs."

Lee nodded. They'd "strongly advised" her to sign a confidentiality waiver. Now they handed her a handsome check.

The pixie's smile suggested she wasn't good with people. "I'm sorry you had to see this. I'm sorry about your friend. If you find Trooper Margolin, he'll be ready to go in a half hour or so."

She liked Margolin, and Margolin had liked Vince. They could share their grief on the drive back. The pixie dismissed her, and stalked off, presumably to threaten the next witness.

36 - MARY BETH

Mary Beth's trailer felt just as big and just as empty as it had the last time she'd been here. She had to break a window to get in, and now the hole was stuffed with towels. Cold air still crept through. She had a big fucking check, and no idea what to do with it. She wrapped herself up in a few extra layers and booted up her computer. She spent hours sifting through chat logs with Dennis, reliving conversations. She'd kept them all. The first one where they'd talked for hours, until he'd declared what they were doing stupid, logged off, and driven to her door. God, they'd talked all night. She'd never known it was possible to miss someone this much.

When she tried to think of the grub-thing, something in her mind shimmied, shuddered, and threatened to break. She'd talked to Angela, and didn't expect to see her around much more. Lee had thanked her for listening, apologized for babbling to her. Even though Lee said she wasn't much of a hugger, Mary Beth had hugged her. Lee had a job, she was pretty, she was everything Mary Beth wasn't.

Inside her head, because she felt too foolish to say it out loud, she asked Dennis what to do. He didn't answer.

She started the game on her computer, and slipped into her character's skin. Friends from around the world, friends she would never know in real life, asked her where she'd been, what was going on.

She didn't tell them. The government couldn't buy her silence, but today wasn't the day to spill it. She fell in with her guild, hurried off on a quest bigger than herself, one with massive ramifications of saving the world.

37 – ANGELA

Angela stared at the numbers on the check, stared at her name on the check. She imagined she wasn't the only one hell-bent on leaving Rocky Rhodes, but this made it so much easier.

"You can never speak of this incident. Never again."

"I won't. I'm leaving here as soon as…as soon as my father's feeling better. And then I'm never coming back."

Maybe she could go farther than Orono and the college. There were other schools. Better schools. She could choose a big city or another small town, anywhere in the country.

Jason approached her after the pixie left. He carried his check, rolled into a tight little tube.

"I'm leaving," she told him.

He gave her a wan smile. "I guessed you might be. University of Maine?"

She shook her head. "I don't think so. Farther. Somewhere else. Any suggestions? You've been all around."

"Mostly military bases. I wouldn't recommend Fayetteville. But I think you'd like Washington."

"You're from there, right?"

He nodded. "Been thinking about heading back for a bit. I think my time in good old Rocky Rhodes is about at its end."

Common sense commanded her to keep her mouth shut. She willed herself not to say another word, certainly not what she said to him next.

"Maybe you could show me around out there? I've never been."

He gaped at her.

"I mean, I don't want to date you. I mean not yet. But I like you, and I like being with you, and maybe someday…" She let her voice trail off. She was a babbling idiot.

He grinned at her. He wasn't *that* much older. And she kind of liked all his tattoos. No, she really liked them. It was Nate who told her how awful they were, told her it meant he wasn't a good person. Nate was jealous, she realized, because he *knew* Jason was a better person.

"I'm happy to show you around. I'll help you find a place, and maybe once we get out there, you'd let me take you to dinner."

"Are you asking me out?"

"Only if you'd like to be asked out."

"I'll tell you in Washington."

"It's a deal."

Angela headed back to her house to check on her father. The slightest smile tugged at the corner of her mouth, and she let it come.

The cold kiss of snow and ice soothed open, gashed wounds. Burns and tears. Most of it was lost, presided over by humans. They erected plastic tents around it, brought blinding lights and agonizing heaters.

But not all. A piece escaped, the lure. The woman in white. At first it crawled, so light it didn't disrupt the fresh-fallen snow. It spent the hateful days when the sun made the temperature rise buried in snow, cradled into ice. It moved north. It didn't know as it crossed a slice of Baxter state park, slinking in the night under Katahdin's shadow. Or when it found the Allagash Wilderness Waterway and followed the mighty river. As it grew stronger, under the sparking white of aurora borealis, it crossed out of Maine, out of the United States, through a thin slice of New Brunswick and into Quebec.

Here it found a new type of lights. Brighter. Closer. And so many of them…

It was stronger now, and with strength came hunger.

TRANSLATED FROM FRENCH
QUEBEC CHRONICLE-TELEGRAPH
FEBRUARY 2, 2015

Residents of Riviere-du-Loup, a small city of 20,000, 206 kilometers to the north have reported a strange rash of disappearances. The missing persons cross all ages, from eight to eighty years old, but the thing they all have in common is their gender. The missing people are predominantly male. Police are baffled, saying they have minimal leads, other than that the missing men and boys were often alone in the snowy fields and farmlands to the south of the city. City officials and family members are offering rewards for information leading to the whereabouts of the missing persons. A city curfew has been enacted, but has done little to stem the rising rate of disappearances. At the time of press, 10 men and boys are currently missing.

ABOUT THE AUTHOR

If it screams, squelches, or bleeds, Kristin Dearborn has probably written about it. She revels in comments like "But you look
so normal…how do you come up with that stuff?" A life-long
New Englander, she aspires to the footsteps of the local masters,
Messrs. King and Lovecraft. When not writing or rotting her
brain with cheesy horror flicks (preferably creature features!)
she can be found scaling rock cliffs, zipping around Vermont on
a motorcycle, or gallivanting around the globe.

Kristin is the author of *Whispers, Stolen Away, Woman in
White, Sacrifice Island*, and *Trinity*. She has also written several
short stories, most recently appearing in *Chopping Block Party:
An Anthology of Suburban Terror, Screaming Cacti*, and *Single Slices
Volume 1*. Learn more about her at www.kristindearborn.com.

Curious about other Crossroad Press books?
Stop by our site:
http://store.crossroadpress.com
We offer quality writing
in digital, audio, and print formats.